THE EXPELLED / THE CALMATIVE /
THE END *with* FIRST LOVE

Christopher Ricks is Professor of the Humanities at Boston
University, and was Professor of Poetry at Oxford, 2004–2009.
He published on Samuel Beckett in 1955, and more recently
(2008) in *Fulcrum*. He edited Beckett's *As the story was told*
(The Rampant Lions Press, 1987), and is the author of
Beckett's Dying Words (Oxford University Press, 1993).

Titles in the Samuel Beckett series

Forthcoming titles

SAMUEL BECKETT

The Expelled
The Calmative
The End
with
First Love

Edited by Christopher Ricks

faber and faber

'The Expelled', 'The End', and 'The Calmative' were collected, after periodical publication, in *Stories and Texts for Nothing* (Grove Press, New York, 1967), and in *No's Knife* (Calder and Boyars, 1967).

In *Collected Shorter Prose 1945–1980* (Calder, London, 1984), the three stories were joined by 'First Love' (*First Love*, Calder, 1973; *First Love and Other Shorts*, Grove, 1974). *The Complete Short Prose, 1929–1989* (Grove, 1995) has all four.

The French originals of the three ('L'Expulsé', 'La Fin', 'Le Calmant') had been collected in *Nouvelles et Textes pour rien* (Les Éditions de Minuit, Paris, 1955). 'Premier Amour' followed (Minuit, 1970).

This edition first published in 2009
by Faber and Faber Ltd
Bloomsbury House
74–77 Great Russell Street
London WC1B 3DA

Typeset byRefineCatch Limited, Bungay, Suffolk
Printed and bound by CPI Group (UK) Ltd, Croydon, CR0 4YY

A CIP record for this book
is available from the British Library

ISBN 978-0-571-24461-4

Contents

Preface

Here are three associated stories, *The Expelled*, *The Calmative*, and *The End*, along with a fourth, *First Love*.

Publication

Beckett's fourfold enterprise hinged pointedly on his turning, a couple of months before he turned forty in 1946, from writing in English to writing in French. The earliest of the stories, the one that was to become *The End*, was begun in English, with a move then to French on the twenty-ninth page of the manuscript (which is now at Boston College).

The later literary world, which had been under the impression that *La Fin* originated in French, learnt of Beckett's midway change-of-mind from James Knowlson's indispensably humane narrative, *Damned to Fame: The Life of Samuel Beckett* (pp.325, 687). When this biography came out in September 1996, Beckett had been dead for nearly seven years. Eerily, on the verso of the title-page, within the Library of Congress Cataloguing-in-Publication Data, Samuel Beckett lives on: *Beckett, Samuel, 1906–*.

Publication began with this story *La Fin*, which appeared – half of it, some mistake surely – with the title *Suite* in *Les Temps modernes* 1:10, 1 July 1946. (*Suite*: 'What Follows'.) Six months later, there followed *L'Expulsé* (subsequently *The Expelled*) in *Fontaine* X:57 (December 1946–January 1947). Revised, these two *nouvelles* were joined eight years later by *Le Calmant* (subsequently *The Calmative*) within *Nouvelles et Textes pour rien* in November 1955.

Now turn to English, the Irishman's stepmother tongue. This began with *The End*, which appeared eight years later than its

French forebear, in *Merlin: A Collection of Contemporary Writing* 2:3, Paris, Summer–Autumn 1954, translated from the French by Richard Seaver in collaboration with the author.[1] (With the printing errors corrected,[2] and revisions by Beckett, it resurfaced six years later in *Evergreen Review* 4:15, New York, November–December 1960.) The next story, *The Expelled*, was in *Evergreen Review* 6:22, January–February 1962, likewise as to collaborative translation. Then, five years later, came *The Calmative* in *Evergreen Review* 11:47, June 1967, this one being translated by the author.[3] Almost simultaneously in 1967, all three stories were published in America within *Stories and Texts for Nothing*.[4]

The French originals, then, were published 1946, 1947, and 1955. Beckett turned fifty in 1956. In English, the stories were published 1954, 1962, and 1967, but in England proper, none until all three in 1967, in *No's Knife: Collected Shorter Prose 1945–1966*. Beckett turned sixty in 1966.

Among the inescapabilities that are faced in the stories is ageing.

In a review of *Nouvelles et Textes pour rien* in 1955, René Lalou in *Les Nouvelles Littéraires* observed that the stories portray three successive stages in the downfall of a human being.[5] The three are given in the present edition in this, the order of the original French collection as well as of their first appearance in England in *No's Knife* and of all subsequent collected volumes during Beckett's lifetime, including the first English gathering of all four stories, *Four Novellas* (1977).[6]

First Love, the fourth story, was off on its own. Beckett was more than usually unhappy with it. It was not until 1970 that *Premier Amour*, '1945', appeared as a very slim book, as did *First Love* at last in England in 1973, translated from the original French by the author, again '1945', and then in America in 1974 within *First Love and Other Shorts*.[7]

Stories was the term corresponding to the French *Nouvelles* when the three were collected in America within *Stories and Texts for Nothing* in 1967, which was also the year when, with the same heading, they were published in England within *No's Knife*. The word *stories* is the better one, given Beckett's title *Stories and Texts for Nothing*, the half-title page in *No's Knife*, and his tables of contents. After the mistitled *Four Novellas*, the stories figured in *Collected Shorter Prose 1945–1980* (1984), and – after Beckett's death which was in 1989 and as the first American inclusion of all four – in *The Complete Short Prose, 1929–1989* (edited by S.E. Gontarski, 1995).

There were far-sighted publishers in Paris, London, and New York. As for Dublin, the Republic of Ireland took some pleasure in his writing, but the pleasure had traditionally been that of banning his books as against publishing them.

Composition

Of *The End*, Beckett jotted down: 'This story (1945) was first text written directly in French.' This was in 1957, and a 1961 jotting is similar: 'This is the translation of the first story I wrote in French (1945?).'[8] As to the original French, which was at first *Suite*, Beckett wrote to his friend George Reavey on 27 May 1946: 'I have finished my French story, about 45:000 words I think. The first half is appearing in the July *Temps modernes* (Sartre's canard).' He added, 'I hope to have the complete story published as a separate work. In France they don't bother counting words. Camus's *Etranger* is not any longer.'[9] Then on 1 September 1946: 'The first part of my story *Suite* has appeared in the July number of the *Temps modernes* and the second and last part will appear in October.'[10]

But this was not to be, for the powers that be (Beauvoir, Simone de) declared that she – and Sartre, in her wake – had imagined that the first half was the whole story. She threw in for bad measure the insistence that anyway the first half of *Suite* was complete in itself and needed no following. Beckett's dignified remonstration to her, when she refused to print the second half of the story, has a revelatory force as to all three stories, and so is postponed in this preface till the end.

The autograph manuscript of the next story, *L'Expulsé*, is dated as having been begun 6 October 1946 and completed 14 October, and that of *Le Calmant* as begun 23 December 1946.

On 15 December 1946, Beckett wrote to Reavey: 'I hope to have a book of short stories ready for the Spring (in French). I do not think I shall write very much in English in the future.'[11] Nearly ten years in the future was his next writing in English, *From an Abandoned Work*: 'This text was written 1954 or 1955. It is the first text written directly in English since *Watt* (1945).'[12] But written *in*directly in English, although assuredly written in direct English, there came the translations of the three stories from the French, after a while. For it was not until November 1953 that Beckett engaged with Richard Seaver on translation of *The End*.[13] (The slovenly printing in *Merlin* was to be corrected and revised in *Evergreen Review*, 1960.) By January 1962, Beckett was revising unfeverishly the Seaverish translation of *The Expelled*, and it was not until September 1966 that Beckett's own translation of *The Calmative* was brought to rest.

First Love is a different story. Beckett began *Premier Amour* on 28 October 1946 and finished it on 12 November. He did not include it in *Nouvelles et Textes pour rien* in 1955, and only in 1969 did he yield to the importunities of his publisher Jérôme Lindon, who was hoping that Beckett would allow a limited edition of the two unpublished works of 1945–46, *Premier Amour* and the novel *Mercier et Camier*.[14] Beckett's winning the Nobel Prize in October 1969 made Lindon redouble his efforts, and Beckett was slowly to acquiesce. (Not the Joycean *ahquickyes*.) *Premier Amour* was published in May 1970. The next month, he wrote that he regretted having ever agreed to publication.[15] The regret went beyond James Knowlson's summing-up, 'He was unhappy at the prospect of releasing work over twenty years old that he no longer liked', for although this would have been bad enough, it wasn't just a matter of *no longer*. Then, having been good to his French publisher, Beckett felt that he had better be good to his English one, and in January 1970 he let Calder know that he would let him issue *First Love*.

In April–May 1971, Beckett sketched something, and exactly a year later he set about writing.[16] By 11 February 1973 he had revised and completed the translation, and for readers in England the first sight of *First Love* came in July 1973. Since it was not till the next year, 1974, that the American edition appeared, it might have been supposed that this latter was later. But the text that had been sent to Grove Press was to find itself revised for Calder, and the English edition includes a good many revisions of this American text that had preceded it except when it came to publication.[17] 'Personally I have no bone to pick with graveyards': so it goes in the English edition (1973). In the American (1974), which is earlier in an Irish way: 'Personally I have nothing against graveyards', a faithful but insufficiently mordant swallowing of the original French: 'Personellement je n'ai rien contre les cimetières.'

Personally: if the stories are to some degree personal, autobiographical, they are so only in the sense that Beckett's experiences went privately to the making of them. The public meaning of them is something else, and somewhere else. That there are memories of his own childhood (his bedroom, the story of Joe Breem or Breen, a cylindrical ruler, the mountains[18]) and of his own travels (the famous cemetery at Ohlsdorf[19]): this can be touching, but what it touches upon is Beckett the man, not the art. For the stories do not call into play these intimations as individually his. James Knowlson writes both eloquently and discriminatingly of the mountainside with its lights:

> Using them purely as undefined memories universalizes them, leaving feelings that are situated somewhere between ache and glow and evoking the closeness of the bond between father and son but not romanticizing it.

Of the narrator's inability in *The End* to recognize any longer the streets of the city, Knowlson observes:

> This passage could almost have come from one of Beckett's

own letters and reflects the experience of his return to Dublin or Paris after the war. But it focuses on the experience of change and the feeling of estrangement that the protagonist feels, not on any specific localities. And so a fictional space is created that is related to the geographical space but has its own more universal validity.[20]

Even more than the validity, it is the value and the values of the locales that may be visualized by the mind's eye in the stories, and that then in the ample picturing of *The Beckett Country* may be seen by the eye of flesh.[21] There in the countryside is the gorse fire on the mountains, and there in the city, the horse-drawn cab and the stone drinking-trough.

First Love is sardonic about the father's grave. ('But my father's yard was not amongst my favourite.') Such is art. Or at least, such is one form or impetus that art may take. *The Beckett Country* is something else, and its photographs are life, and are death.

SACRED

TO THE MEMORY OF

WILLIAM FRANK BECKETT

DIED 26TH JUNE 1933

AGED 61 YEARS,

AND OF HIS WIFE

MARY

DIED 25TH AUGUST 1950

AGED 75 YEARS.

AGED 61 YEARS: Samuel Beckett was to become this age in 1967, the year in which the three stories first appeared in England. This is no more than a coincidence, as of course is the fact that the year in which Beckett's father died is the year in which I was born. But they make you think, these things, as do these telling stories.

Reception

In 1952, Richard Seaver introduced Beckett to the readers of *Merlin* (published in Paris) in terms that were immediately to the point: 'Samuel Beckett, an Irish writer long established in France, has recently published two novels which, although they defy all commentary, merit the attention of anyone interested in this century's literature.' The two novels in French were *Molloy* and *Malone meurt*, both 1951. Seaver, after informing (hardly reminding) his readers that Beckett had published in England in 1934 a volume of short stories, *More Pricks than Kicks*, and in 1938 a novel, *Murphy*, addressed one of the three stories in French that he, Seaver, was to assist in various ways. '*L'Expulsé* tells of a man, more world-weary than Murphy, who is ejected from his lodgings for an unexplained and no doubt unexplainable reason.'[22] Its hero, if that is the word (and oddly it is), is 'the same deadbeat as in "Suite"' (Beckett, to Reavey). Carlton Lake has called *L'Expulsé* 'Beckett's world in microcosm and a masterpiece of the short story'.[23]

Samuel Beckett: The Critical Heritage does not bequeath much to us by way of reviews of *Nouvelles et Textes pour rien* (1955),[24] or of *Stories and Texts for Nothing* and *No's Knife* (the American and English appearances in 1967). Specific notice of the stories is largely absent. But a present writer takes a small pride in having picked out in a review 'the three superb stories' that Beckett wrote in 1945–46: 'they are Beckett at his very best, witty, unpredictable, and desperately poignant. *The End* is the best possible introduction to Beckett's fiction.'[25] It was less the immediate reviewers who illuminated the art than the later critics, and of these the most venturesome of all Beckett's appreciators, Hugh Kenner. 'As being his first venture in the mode he was to exploit so richly, the three *Stories* repay close attention.'

In all three a narrator, always on the move, is struggling with the superficies of mundane existence, shelter, food, diversion; not striving to execute any specific purpose, but staying alive because he is alive.

In addition to the first person and its vagaries – the inability to remember facts, the uncertainty as to why he is narrating at all, the loss of heart when set-pieces seem called for ('Only the ground-floor windows—no, I can't') – two other Beckett conventions at least are introduced: the narrator's gradual reduction to vagrancy, and the semblance of his world to that of silent films.

All that happens in the first is a day spent wandering and a night spent in a stable, and led on though we are irresistibly from sentence to sentence, we are not prevented from reflecting that nothing more happens. All that happens in the second, which seems to entail a spell of hospitalization, is a bedridden man's story of encounters that seem hallucinatory and close amid a swoon with the lucidity of hallucination. All that happens in the third is an indigent's progress toward that leaking boat. The three span a descent from middle-class somnambulistic orthodoxy to the fluid expedients of beggardom, traversed with neither surprise nor rancour, and with never a backward glance.[26]

'The three': but there were to be four, when *The Expelled*, *The Calmative*, and *The End* found themselves in undue course accompanied by *First Love*, a story in which Beckett did not believe, for he did not believe that he had found himself or anything else much. When *First Love* was first published in 1973, this reviewer for one was sure that Beckett had judged aright, and I said roundly and squarely that 'He was right to reject it; its disgust is factitious and its heartlessness is not heartfelt. There is hardly anything in it which Beckett has not more deeply and more exactly effected elsewhere.'[27] Now I am not so sure, or rather, am sure that I fell far short of doing justice to a Beckett story that does itself fall short but is a thousand times better than you or I could do. It is with some relief that I now draw ineffectual attention to a small room for manoeuvre that I entered in 1973 (*There is hardly anything in it which* . . .). It is with a touch more relief that I recall where I then turned: 'It will matter only to those to whom Beckett already greatly matters, and what will probably most interest them is Beckett's way of translating it from his original French.'

Beckett continually encourages the English language to betray the glorious inappositeness of its casual clichés. So *à sa place* becomes *in her shoes*. 'I in her shoes would have tiptoed away, but not she, not a stir.' For a split second, you glimpse the puzzled old man perched in a woman's shoes, the effect teetering upon the absence of any liaison of sound from 'I' to 'in'; not 'In her shoes I would have tiptoed away', but 'I in her shoes'. There is something fetching and childlike about the frozen gait: 'but not she, not a stir'. Robert Louis Stevenson, *A Child's Garden of Verses*: 'Not a stir of child or mouse.' Again, for *pas la première fois que je voyais une femme nue*, Beckett transforms any straightforward English (such as 'not the first time that I saw a naked woman') into the weirdly wonderful: 'Fortunately she was not the first naked woman to have crossed my path, so I could stay, I knew she would not explode.'[28]

Such are the happy infelicities that cross our path in *First Love* as against *Premier Amour*. But there was something negligent about my disaccord (and I failed to attend to it), the discrepancy between my all-but-dismissing the story and the welcoming with which my review opened:

> From first to last, Samuel Beckett has been indeflectible, as high narrow genius is. From *First Love*, which he wrote twenty-eight years ago in French, to *Not I*, his recent play in which a stricken illuminated mouth is 'flickering away like mad', he has shown a grimly impressive obduracy of preoccupation, a gripping clutch of interests. His characters, too, are indeflectible. The cracked and cackling narrator of *First Love* – who tells of how he met a woman on a bench,

went back to live with her, and left her as she was giving birth to his child – has all the pertinacity of that bone-deep fatigue which gives Beckett's decrepit figures (ruined leech-gatherers) their ruthless strength, their rigour, not mortis but of moribundity.

When someone asked if he was English, Beckett the Irishman legendarily replied, 'Au contraire.' When he creates anew a French story as one in English, or the other way round, he is quite contrary. For whereas there are no structural differences between the stories when in French and when in English, and there are not many cuts or graftings (a few sentences here and there), there is a continual play of mind and of emotion at all the local levels and swivels.

The End

So back to *The End*. In 1946, Simone de Beauvoir, it will be remembered, had made out that *Suite* was entire, whereas it really was only half the story; that even if it weren't the whole story, it now would have to be, as far as *Les Temps modernes* was concerned (that is, not far); and that Beckett had been disingenuous. Beckett's reply to her is marked by the studied propriety that characterized Dr Johnson's lethal letter to a false patron of his, the lofty Lord Chesterfield. Beckett's letter, although and because it takes us back to the story of how these stories started, is the right place to end yet again.

Simone de Beauvoir had seen to it that *Suite/La Fin* would come to an end with the words 'au delà du stupide espoir de repos ou de moindre peine': 'But the day came when, looking round me, I was in the suburbs, and from there to the old haunts it was not far, beyond the stupid hope of rest or less pain.'

He wrote to her, in French, on 25 September 1946:[29]

I regret this misunderstanding which puts you under the obligation of stopping my story mid-way [*à mi-chemin*]. The regret is that of a victim.

You are thinking of the standing [*la bonne tenue*] of your periodical. This is natural. For my part, I am thinking of the person/character [*personnage*] in *Suite* frustrated of his repose/rest [*repos*]. This, too, is natural, I think. It is with difficulty that I put myself in your place, since I understand nothing about matters of editing. But I have read your books, and know that you can put yourself in my place.

I should not wish you to mistake the intention [*sens*] of this letter, which I write only after long hesitation. I have no wish for debate. I am not asking you to go back into/upon [*revenir sur*] what you have decided. But it is decidedly impossible for me to doff [*de me dérober au*] the duty that I feel towards a created being [*une créature*]. Forgive these high-sounding words. If I were afraid of ridicule, I should remain silent.

I have enough confidence in you to tell you quite simply what I feel. Here it is. You grant me leave to speak, only to rescind it before it has time to mean anything. You bring to a halt a state of being on the threshold of its realization. [*Vous immobilisez une existence au seuil de sa solution.*] This has about it something nightmarish [*cauchemardesque*]. I find it painful to believe that concern for presentation [*livre de bonne présentation* = a well-produced book] could justify in your eyes such a mutilation.

You think that the fragment that appeared in your last number is a finished thing [*une chose achevée*]. This is not my judgment. It is only a major premise.

Do not be angry at this frankness. [*Ne m'en voulez*, for *veuillez*.] It is without rancour. There is a destitution/ extreme poverty/misery [*misère*] that must be championed/defended [*qu'il faut défendre*] to the end, in one's work and outside one's work.

From the beginning to the end, Beckett's letter is alive not only to this particular story, *La Fin/The End*, but to the other stories soon to ensue. The mutilation by *Les Temps modernes* broke off here:

'from there to the old haunts it was not far, beyond the stupid hope of rest or less pain'. Beckett urged in reply a hope that was not stupid, and he refused to let the matter rest. More pain, not less, had to be contemplated. It is neither the story's creator alone who is in danger of being frustrated of rest and of repose, nor the created being alone, *une créature*, but the two of them.

Beckett's stories engage all this. What it is to be forced to stop mid-way. To be a victim. To be frustrated of rest and of repose. To make the effort to put oneself in another's place. To go back into – or go back upon – something. To throw something off (*de me dérober*), within these stories that imagine with such precise pain what clothes are – say, the clothes of a dead man that now a moribund man has to don, at the start of *The Expelled*. Or, in *First Love*, the clothes abruptly doffed: 'She began to undress. When at their wit's end they undress, no doubt the wisest course. She took off everything, with a slowness fit to enflame an elephant, except her stockings, calculated presumably to bring my concupiscence to the boil. It was then I noticed the squint.'

To be granted leave to speak and then to have it rescinded. To be brought to a halt, immobilized. To be prevented from crossing a threshold. What nightmare is, or mutilation, destitution. In a word, misery.

THE TEXT

The text here is that of the last edition in Beckett's lifetime, *Collected Shorter Prose 1945–1980* (1984). No corrections to this are needed for *The Expelled*. For *The End*, 'sometime' has been corrected to 'some time', and for *The Calmative* 'and end' to 'an end', and 'lengthens. Stiffens' to 'lengthens, stiffens'.

With *First Love*, the 1984 text often diverges from the 1973 (English) publication or from the 1974 (American) one.[30] Some of the discrepancies are 1984 slips: the correct reading is not 1984 *partially thanks to* but 1973/1974 *partially, thanks to*; not 1984 *hung together* but 1973/1974 *clung together*; not 1984/1973 *that on its* but 1974 *than on its*; not 1984 *utrica* but 1973/1974 *urtica*; not 1984 *later even more* but 1973/1974 *later, even more*; not 1984 *mantlepiece* but 1973/1974 *mantelpiece*; not 1984 *doen't* but *doesn't*. On the other hand, there are the cases where 1984 is almost certainly right to depart from 1973/1974. Not 1973/1974 *nettles, some full three foot high* but 1984 *nettles some full three foot high*. Not 1973/1974 *cowplats* but 1984 *cowpats*. (Dukes points out that Beckett marked the change to *cowpats* on a set of corrected proofs for 1984.) Not 1973/1974 *To put it wildly* (enticing though this is, for a wild moment) but 1984 *mildly*. Not 1973 *the idea every* but 1974/1984 *the idea, every*.

This leaves a handful ('To divellicate urtica *plenibus manibus*?') where an editor must seize the nettle.

First, I retain 1984 *But my father's yard was not amongst my favourite*. Gontarski says that 1974 *among my favourite* was changed in 1984 to *amongst my favourites*, the wording that he adopts. (No, 1984 has *amongst my favourite*; 1973/1974 *among my favourite*.) Dukes concurs with Gontarski, *amongst my favourites*, 'because conventional usage favours a plural noun following the preposition *amongst*'. But this emendation is unwarranted, for 1984 *amongst my favourite* (like 1973 *among my favourite*) offers *favourite* not as a noun but as an adjective, so that *amongst my favourite* [*graveyards*] has a flat-tongued touch of class and drawl: *But my father's yard was not amongst my favourite*.

Second, I retain 1973/1984: *he had stipulated in his will that I be left the room I had occupied in his lifetime and food brought me there, as hitherto*. Dukes and Gontarski follow 1974: *and for food to be brought me there*. But the twofold stipulation was *that I be left the room I had occupied in his lifetime and food brought me there, as hitherto.* This is aptly stiff and legalistic, whereas 'stipulated for food to be brought' (stipulate *for*?) is merely ungainly.

Third, I retain 1984 *at home, at school*, not 1973/1974 *at home, in school*, though the latter is preferred by Dukes and Gontarski for its not varying the symmetrical pattern of the prepositions in previous printings: *at . . . in . . . in . . . at*. (Might not Beckett have come to distrust the sway of such symmetry?)

xix

Fourth, Gontarski retains, as I do, the punctuation of 1973/1984 *But why these particulars*. Period. Dukes follows 1974 (adducing the punctuation in the French): *But why these particulars?* He points out that the question-mark is only partially visible in the second typescript. But more telling than the inflection of *But why these particulars?* is the level bathos of 1984: *But why these particulars*. Not really a question, the weary full-stop acknowledges.

Finally, there is an occasion where Dukes and Gontarski follow 1984, as I ordinarily do, but where I revert to 1973/1974, which – like the French original – has the following exchange:

> My stewpan, she said. I don't need the lid, I said. You don't need the lid? she said. If I had said I needed the lid she would have said, You need the lid?

1984 reduces *If I had said I needed*, down to *If I had needed*, an excision that loosens those teeth clenched in the face of the maddening. (Earlier in the story: 'It's incredible the way they repeat what you've just said to them, as if they risked faggot and fire in believing their ears.') So I follow 1973/1974, aware both that 1984 does makes sense and that its doing so might explain why nobody noticed that *If I had said* was no longer being said.

Notes

1 *No Symbols Where None Intended: A Catalogue of Books, Manuscripts, and Other Material Relating to Samuel Beckett in the Collections of the Humanities Research Center* (the University of Texas at Austin, 1984), selected and described by Carlton Lake. Lake observes of items 173, 174: 'Although Beckett is listed here as collaborator, the translation would appear to be Seaver's own, to judge from the account he has given' in *I can't go on, I'll go on* (1976); it is the translation in *Evergreen Review* 1960 that 'would seem to be the one that resulted from the Beckett–Seaver collaboration'.

2 Beckett deplored the fact that, 'for want of proof correction', the *Merlin* publication was 'full of ridiculous mistakes'. To Alexander Trocchi, 27 August 1954; *Damned to Fame*, p. 358. The contents page for *Merlin* 1:2, Autumn 1952, had failed better, by misspelling the name Beckett.

3 Incorporated were two of the six drawings by Avigdor Arikha that had been in the second, 1958, edition of *Nouvelles et Textes pour rien*.

4 *No Symbols Where None Intended*, item 179, gives the *Evergreen Review* publication (June 1967) as 'just prior to' *Stories and Texts for Nothing*; item 190 is a presentation copy of *Stories and Texts for Nothing* from Beckett in March 1967.

5 A translation of this review is in *Samuel Beckett: The Critical Heritage*, eds., Lawrence Graver and Raymond Federman (1979), pp. 137–9.

6 *First Love and Other Novellas* (edited by Gerry Dukes, Penguin, 2000) gives the three stories in the order of the initial publication of each: *The End, The Expelled, The Calmative*, followed by *First Love*, tilting the title *First Love and Other Novellas*. Dukes has a dozen pages of very rewarding notes on manuscript revisions, English/American textual variants, and French/English variations.

7 S.E. Gontarski, in *The Complete Short Prose, 1929–1989* (1995), puts *First Love* first, following the order in *Collected Shorter Prose 1945–1980* (1984). But *Premier Amour/First Love* was not the first of the stories to be written, and Beckett's decades of dissatisfaction with it, together with the fact that the three previously published stories not only constituted a remarkable inauguration of his later genius but are linked (albeit loosely), are the grounds for overriding 1984 in the present edition (as did Dukes) and putting *First Love* last, appended.

8 First *story*, for he had started to write poems in French even before the war. Manuscript and other evidence establishes 1946 as the year of composition for all the stories. But Beckett did inscribe *The End* '1945' and '1945?', with *Premier Amour/First Love* dated '1945'. Moreover, there is the *Note de l'Editeur* in *Nouvelles et Textes pour rien* (1955): 'Les *Nouvelles* sont de 1945, les *Textes pour rien* de 1950.' But with the further wrinkle that Les Éditions de Minuit, listing its titles, gave *Nouvelles et Textes pour rien (1946–1950)*. In so often giving '1945', Beckett may have been recalling when he set his mind to work, as against his pen to paper.

9 *La Fin /The End* is about 10,000 words. 'About 45:000 words I think': what can Beckett have been thinking? Or writing? The figure is remarkable, though unremarked by Lake or Knowlson. Even if Beckett were thinking of the first half only (which was all that he sent to *Les Temps modernes* at first), with its possibility of *4,500* words, there would still be the fact that Camus's *L'Etranger* is a book of about 28,000 words. Might 45,000 words have been Beckett's loose guess at the tot of all three stories? But then the letter to Reavey precludes this: 'I have finished my French story, about 45:000 words I think. The first half is appearing in the July *Temps Modernes*.'

10 *Damned to Fame*, p. 325. See *No Symbols Where None Intended*, where the holdings of the stories occupy pp. 81–5, items 172–6, 178–9, 198; 175 is a manuscript of *L'Expulsé* , and 179 of *Le Calmant*. A manuscript of *La Fin* is at Boston College; *The Calmative*, manuscript and typescript, at the Olin

Library, Washington University; *First Love*, manuscript and typescript, at Reading University.

11 *No Symbols Where None Intended*, p. 81 (headnote to the section on *Stories and Texts for Nothing*).

12 *No Symbols Where None Intended*, item 198.

13 See *A Samuel Beckett Chronology* (2006), a scrupulously valuable facilitator from the hand and mind of John Pilling.

14 *Damned to Fame*, p. 498, Lindon's letter of 16 December 1968.

15 *Damned to Fame*, pp. 509, 512, 726, to Josette Hayden.

16 Dated 24 April 1972–18 May 1972, the manuscript is at Reading.

17 S.E. Gontarski gives some lively instances in his Note on the Texts, *The Complete Short Prose*, pp. 280–1.

18 *Damned to Fame*, pp. 336–8.

19 Beckett visited it in 1936; *Damned to Fame*, pp. 224–5.

20 *Damned to Fame*, p. 338.

21 "The eye of flesh": the words of *The Expelled*, from Job 10:4, "Hast thou eyes of flesh?" Eoin O'Brien, *The Beckett Country* (1986), the photography of David H. Davison, pp. 58–9, 72, 212, 263.

22 'Samuel Beckett: An Introduction', *Merlin* 1:2, Autumn 1952; *Beckett: The Critical Heritage*, p. 79.

23 *No Symbols Where None Intended*, item 176.

24 The reviews of *Nouvelles et Textes pour rien* by René Lalou (22 December 1955) and by Geneviève Bonnefoi (March 1956) are translated in *Beckett: The Critical Heritage*, pp. 137–45.

25 Christopher Ricks, *The Listener* (3 August 1967); *Beckett: The Critical Heritage*, pp. 286–90.

26 *A Reader's Guide to Samuel Beckett* (1973), pp. 116–18.

27 *Sunday Times* (15 July 1973).

28 Here I draw on my book *Beckett's Dying Words* (1993), pp. 64–6.

29 The letter appears in *No Symbols Where None Intended*, pp. 81–2. The translation of Beckett's French is mine, and cannot but fall short.

30 On the time-warp by which 1973 is a revision of 1974, see earlier in this Preface.

Table of Dates

Where unspecified, translations from French to English or vice versa are by Beckett.

1906
13 April   Samuel Beckett [Samuel Barclay Beckett] born in 'Cooldrinagh', a house in Foxrock, a village south of Dublin, on Good Friday, the second child of William Beckett and May Beckett, née Roe; he is preceded by a brother, Frank Edward, born 26 July 1902.

1911
            Enters kindergarten at Ida and Pauline Elsner's private academy in Leopardstown.

1915
            Attends larger Earlsfort House School in Dublin.

1920
            Follows Frank to Portora Royal, a distinguished Protestant boarding school in Enniskillen, County Fermanagh (soon to become part of Northern Ireland).

1923
October   Enrols at Trinity College Dublin (TCD) to study for an Arts degree.

1926
August   First visit to France, a month-long cycling tour of the Loire Valley.

1927
April–August Travels through Florence and Venice, visiting museums, galleries, and churches.

December   Receives B.A. in Modern Languages (French and Italian) and graduates first in the First Class.

1928

Jan.–June	Teaches French and English at Campbell College, Belfast.
September	First trip to Germany to visit seventeen-year-old Peggy Sinclair, a cousin on his father's side, and her family in Kassel.
1 November	Arrives in Paris as an exchange *lecteur* at the École Normale Supérieure. Quickly becomes friends with his predecessor, Thomas McGreevy [after 1943, MacGreevy], who introduces Beckett to James Joyce and other influential anglophone writers and publishers.
December	Spends Christmas in Kassel (as also in 1929, 1930 and 1931).

1929

June	Publishes first critical essay ('Dante . . . Bruno . Vico . . Joyce') and first story ('Assumption') in *transition* magazine.

1930

July	*Whoroscope* (Paris: Hours Press).
October	Returns to TCD to begin a two-year appointment as lecturer in French.
November	Introduced by MacGreevy to the painter and writer Jack B. Yeats in Dublin.

1931

March	*Proust* (London: Chatto and Windus).
September	First Irish publication, the poem 'Alba' in *Dublin Magazine*.

1932

January	Resigns his lectureship via telegram from Kassel and moves to Paris.
Feb.–June	First serious attempt at a novel, the posthumously published *Dream of Fair to Middling Women*.
December	Story 'Dante and the Lobster' appears in *This Quarter* (Paris).

1933

3 May	Death of Peggy Sinclair from tuberculosis.
26 June	Death of William Beckett from a heart attack.

1934

January	Moves to London and begins psychoanalysis with Wilfred Bion at the Tavistock Clinic.
February	*Negro Anthology*, edited by Nancy Cunard and with numerous translations by Beckett from the French (London: Wishart and Company).
May	*More Pricks Than Kicks* (London: Chatto and Windus).
Aug.–Sept.	Contributes several stories and reviews to literary magazines in London and Dublin.

1935

November	*Echo's Bones and Other Precipitates*, a cycle of thirteen poems (Paris: Europa Press).

1936

	Returns to Dublin.
29 September	Leaves Ireland for a seven-month stay in Germany.

1937

Apr.–Aug.	First serious attempt at a play, *Human Wishes*, about Samuel Johnson and his household.
October	Settles in Paris.

1938

6/7 January	Stabbed by a street pimp in Montparnasse. Among his visitors at Hôpital Broussais is Suzanne Deschevaux-Dumesnil, an acquaintance who is to become Beckett's companion for life.
March	*Murphy* (London: Routledge).
April	Begins writing poetry directly in French.

1939

3 September	Great Britain and France declare war on Germany. Beckett abruptly ends a visit to Ireland and returns to Paris the next day.

1940

June　　　　　Travels south with Suzanne following the Fall of France, as part of the exodus from the capital.

September　　Returns to Paris.

1941

13 January　　Death of James Joyce in Zurich.

1 September　Joins the Resistance cell Gloria SMH.

1942

16 August　　Goes into hiding with Suzanne after the arrest of close friend Alfred Péron.

6 October　　Arrival at Roussillon, a small village in unoccupied southern France.

1944

24 August　　Liberation of Paris.

1945

30 March　　Awarded the Croix de Guerre.

Aug.–Dec.　Volunteers as a storekeeper and interpreter with the Irish Red Cross in Saint-Lô, Normandy.

1946

July　　　　Publishes first fiction in French – a truncated version of the short story 'Suite' (later to become 'La Fin') in *Les Temps modernes*, owing to a misunderstanding by editors – as well as a critical essay on Dutch painters Geer and Bram van Velde in *Cahiers d'art*.

1947

Jan.–Feb.　Writes first play, in French, *Eleutheria* (published posthumously).

April　　　*Murphy*, French translation (Paris: Bordas).

1948

　　　　　Undertakes a number of translations commissioned by UNESCO and by Georges Duthuit.

1950

25 August   Death of May Beckett.

1951

March   *Molloy*, in French (Paris: Les Éditions de
                Minuit).

November   *Malone meurt* (Paris: Minuit).

1952

                Purchases land at Ussy-sur-Marne,
                subsequently Beckett's preferred location for
                writing.

September   *En attendant Godot* (Paris: Minuit).

1953

5 January   Premiere of *Godot* at the Théâtre de Babylone
                in Montparnasse, directed by Roger Blin.

May   *L'Innommable* (Paris: Minuit).

August   *Watt*, in English (Paris: Olympia Press).

1954

8 September   *Waiting for Godot* (New York: Grove Press).

13 September   Death of Frank Beckett from lung cancer.

1955

March   *Molloy*, translated into English with Patrick
                Bowles (New York: Grove; Paris: Olympia).

3 August   First English production of *Godot* opens in
                London at the Arts Theatre.

November   *Nouvelles et Textes pour rien* (Paris: Minuit).

1956

3 January   American *Godot* premiere in Miami.

February   First British publication of *Waiting for Godot*
                (London: Faber).

October   *Malone Dies* (New York: Grove).

1957

January   First radio broadcast, *All That Fall* on the
                BBC Third Programme.
                Fin de partie, suivi de Acte sans paroles (Paris:
                Minuit).

28 March   Death of Jack B. Yeats.

May	Assists with the German production of *Play* (*Spiel*, translated by Elmar and Erika Tophoven) in Ulm.
22 May	Outline of *Film* sent to Grove Press. *Film* would be produced in 1964, starring Buster Keaton, and released at the Venice Film Festival the following year.

1964

March	*Play and Two Short Pieces for Radio* (London: Faber).
April	*How It Is*, translation of *Comment c'est* (London: Calder; New York: Grove).
June	*Comédie*, translation of *Play*, in *Les Lettres nouvelles*.
July–Aug.	First and only trip to the United States, to assist with the production of *Film* in New York.

1965

October	*Imagination morte imaginez* (Paris: Minuit).
November	*Imagination Dead Imagine* (London: *The Sunday Times*; Calder).

1966

January	*Comédie et Actes divers*, including *Dis Joe* and *Va et vient* (Paris: Minuit).
February	*Assez* (Paris: Minuit).
October	*Bing* (Paris: Minuit).

1967

February	*D'un ouvrage abandonné* (Paris: Minuit). *Têtes-mortes* (Paris: Minuit).
16 March	Death of Thomas MacGreevy.
June	*Eh Joe and Other Writings*, including *Act Without Words II* and *Film* (London: Faber).
July	*Come and Go*, English translation of *Va et vient* (London: Calder).
26 September	Directs first solo production, *Endspiel* (translation of *Endgame* by Elmar Tophoven) in Berlin.

| November | *No's Knife: Collected Shorter Prose 1945–1966* (London: Calder). |
| December | *Stories and Texts for Nothing*, illustrated with six ink line drawings by Avigdor Arikha (New York: Grove). |

1968

| March | *Poèmes* (Paris: Minuit). |
| December | *Watt*, translated into French with Ludovic and Agnès Janvier (Paris: Minuit). |

1969

| 23 October | Awarded the Nobel Prize for Literature. *Sans* (Paris: Minuit). |

1970

April	*Mercier et Camier* (Paris: Minuit). *Premier amour* (Paris: Minuit).
July	*Lessness*, translation of *Sans* (London: Calder).
September	*Le Dépeupleur* (Paris: Minuit).

1972

| January | *The Lost Ones*, translation of *Le Dépeupleur* (London: Calder; New York: Grove). *The North*, part of *The Lost Ones*, illustrated with etchings by Arikha (London: Enitharmon Press). |

1973

| January | *Not I* (London: Faber). |
| July | *First Love* (London: Calder). |

1974

| | *Mercier and Camier* (London: Calder). |

1975

| Spring | Directs *Godot* in Berlin and *Pas moi* (translation of *Not I*) in Paris. |

1976

| February | *Pour finir encore et autres foirades* (Paris: Minuit). |
| 20 May | Directs Billie Whitelaw in *Footfalls*, which is performed with *That Time* at London's Royal |

	production of *Godot*, directed by Walter Asmus, in London.
	Collected Shorter Plays (London: Faber; New York: Grove).
May	*Collected Poems 1930–1978* (London: Calder).
July	*Collected Shorter Prose 1945–1980* (London: Calder).

1989

April	*Stirrings Still*, with illustrations by Louis le Brocquy (New York: Blue Moon Books).
June	*Nohow On: Company, Ill Seen Ill Said, Worstward Ho*, illustrated with etchings by Robert Ryman (New York: Limited Editions Club).
17 July	Death of Suzanne Beckett.
22 December	Death of Samuel Beckett. Burial in Cimetière de Montparnasse.

★

1990

As the Story Was Told: Uncollected and Late Prose (London: Calder; New York: Riverrun Press).

1992

Dream of Fair to Middling Women (Dublin: Black Cat Press).

1995

Eleutheria (Paris: Minuit).

1996

Eleutheria, translated into English by Barbara Wright (London: Faber).

1998

No Author Better Served: The Correspondence of Samuel Beckett and Alan Schneider, edited by Maurice Harmon (Cambridge MA: Harvard University Press).

2000

Beckett on Film: nineteen films, by different directors, of Beckett's works for the stage (RTÉ, Channel 4, and Irish Film Board; DVD, London: Clarence Pictures).

2006

Samuel Beckett: Works for Radio: The Original Broadcasts: five works spanning the period 1957–1976 (CD, London: British Library Board).

2009

The Letters of Samuel Beckett 1929–1940, edited by Martha Dow Fehsenfeld and Lois More Overbeck (Cambridge: Cambridge University Press).

Compiled by Cassandra Nelson

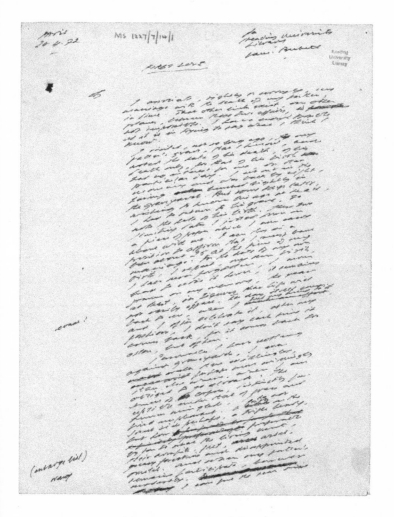

Original manuscript of *First Love*
Courtesy of the Beckett International Foundation, University of Reading.
© The Estate of Samuel Beckett.

The Expelled

There were not many steps. I had counted them a thousand times, both going up and coming down, but the figure has gone from my mind. I have never known whether you should say one with your foot on the sidewalk, two with the following foot on the first step, and so on, or whether the sidewalk shouldn't count. At the top of the steps I fell foul of the same dilemma. In the other direction, I mean from top to bottom, it was the same, the word is not too strong. I did not know where to begin nor where to end, that's the truth of the matter. I arrived therefore at three totally different figures, without ever knowing which of them was right. And when I say that the figure has gone from my mind, I mean that none of the three figures is with me any more, in my mind. It is true that if I were to find, in my mind, where it is certainly to be found, one of these figures, I would find it and it alone, without being able to deduce from it the other two. And even were I to recover two, I would not know the third. No, I would have to find all three, in my mind, in order to know all three. Memories are killing. So you must not think of certain things, of those that are dear to you, or rather you must think of them, for if you don't there is the danger of finding them, in your mind, little by little. That is to say, you must think of them for a while, a good while, every day several times a day, until they sink forever in the mud. That's an order.

After all it is not the number of steps that matters. The important thing to remember is that there were not many, and that I have remembered. Even for the child there were not many, compared to other steps he knew, from seeing them every day, from going up them and coming down, and playing on them at knucklebones and other games the very names of which he has forgotten. What must it have been like then for the man I had overgrown into?

The fall was therefore not serious. Even as I fell I heard the door slam, which brought me a little comfort, in the midst of my fall. For that meant they were not pursuing me down into the street with a stick, to beat me in full view of the passers-by. For if that had been their intention they would not have shut the door, but left it open, so that the persons assembled in the vestibule might enjoy my chastisement and be edified. So, for once, they had confined themselves to throwing me out and no more about it. I had time, before coming to rest in the gutter, to conclude this piece of reasoning.

Under these circumstances nothing compelled me to get up immediately. I rested my elbow on the sidewalk, funny the things you remember, settled my ear in the cup of my hand and began to reflect on my situation, notwithstanding its familiarity. But the sound, fainter but unmistakable, of the door slammed again, roused me from my reverie, in which already a whole landscape was taking form, charming with hawthorn and wild roses, most dreamlike, and made me look up in alarm, my hands flat on the sidewalk and my legs braced for flight. But it was merely my hat sailing towards me through the air, rotating as it came. I caught it and put it on. They were most correct, according to their god. They could have kept this hat, but it was not theirs, it was mine, so they gave it back to me. But the spell was broken.

How describe this hat? And why? When my head had attained I shall not say its definitive but its maximum dimensions, my father said to me, Come, son, we are going to buy your hat, as though it had pre-existed from time immemorial in a pre-established place. He went straight to the hat. I personally had no say in the matter, nor had the hatter. I have often wondered if my father's purpose was not to humiliate me, if he was not jealous of me who was young and handsome, fresh at least, while he was already old and all bloated and purple. It was forbidden me, from that day forth, to go out bareheaded, my pretty brown hair blowing in the wind. Sometimes, in a secluded street, I took it off and held it in my hand, but trembling. I was required to brush it morning and evening. Boys my age with whom, in spite of everything, I was obliged to mix occasionally, mocked me. But I said to myself, It is not really the hat, they simply make merry at the hat because it is a little more glaring than the rest, for they have no finesse. I have always been amazed at my contemporaries' lack of finesse, I whose soul writhed from morning to night, in the mere quest of itself. But perhaps they were simply being kind, like those who make game of the hunchback's big nose. When my father died I could have got rid of this hat, there was nothing more to prevent me, but not I. But how describe it? Some other time, some other time.

I got up and set off. I forget how old I can have been. In what had just happened to me there was nothing in the least memorable. It was neither the cradle nor the grave of anything whatever. Or rather it resembled so many other cradles, so many other graves, that I'm lost. But I don't believe I exaggerate when I say that I was in the prime of life, what I believe is called the full possession of one's faculties. Ah yes, them I possessed all right. I crossed the street and turned back towards the house that had just ejected me, I who never turned back when leaving. How beautiful it was! There were geraniums in the windows. I have brooded over geraniums for years. Geraniums are artful customers, but in the end I was able to do what I liked with them. I have always greatly admired the door of this house, up on top of its little flight of steps. How describe it? It was a massive green door, encased in summer in a kind of green and white striped housing, with a hole for the thunderous wrought-iron knocker and a slit for letters, this latter closed to dust, flies and tits by a brass flap fitted with springs. So much for that description. The door was set between two pillars of the same colour, the bell being on that to the right. The curtains were in unexceptionable taste. Even the smoke rising from one of the chimney-pots seemed to spread and vanish in the air more sorrowful than the neighbours', and bluer. I looked up at the third and last floor and saw my window outrageously open. A thorough cleansing was in full swing. In a few hours they would close the window, draw the curtains and spray the whole place with disinfectant. I knew them. I would have gladly died in that house. In a sort of vision I saw the door open and my feet come out.

I wasn't afraid to look, for I knew they were not spying on me from behind the curtains, as they could have done if they had wished. But I knew them. They had all gone back into their dens and resumed their occupations.

And yet I had done them no harm.

I did not know the town very well, scene of my birth and of my first steps in this world, and then of all the others, so many that I thought all trace of me was lost, but I was wrong. I went out so little! Now and then I would go to the window, part the curtains and look out. But then I hastened back to the depths of the room, where the bed was. I felt ill at ease with all this air about me, lost before the confusion of innumerable prospects. But I still knew how to act at this period, when it was absolutely necessary. But first I raised my eyes to the sky, whence cometh our help, where there are no roads, where you wander freely, as in a desert, and where nothing obstructs your vision, wherever you turn your eyes, but the limits of vision itself. When I was younger I thought life would be good in the middle of a plain and went to the Lüneburg heath. With the plain in my head I went to the heath. There were other heaths far less remote, but a voice kept saying to me, It's the Lüneburg heath you need. The element lüne must have had something to do with it. As it turned out the Lüneburg heath was most unsatisfactory, most unsatisfactory. I came home disappointed and at the same time relieved. Yes, I don't know why, but I have never been disappointed, and I often was in the early days, without feeling at the same time, or a moment later, an undeniable relief.

I set off. What a gait. Stiffness of the lower limbs, as if nature had denied me knees, extraordinary splaying of the feet to right and left of the line of march. The trunk, on the contrary, as if by the effect of a compensatory mechanism, was as flabby as an old ragbag, tossing wildly to the unpredictable jolts of the pelvis. I have often tried to correct these defects, to stiffen my bust, flex my knees and walk with my feet in front of one another, for I had at least five or six, but it always ended in the same way, I mean by a loss of equilibrium, followed by a fall. A man must walk without paying attention to what he's doing, as he sighs, and when I walked without paying attention to what I was doing I walked in the way I have just described, and when I began to pay attention I managed a few steps of creditable execution and then fell. I decided therefore to be myself. This carriage is due, in my opinion, in part at least, to a certain leaning from which I have never been able to free myself completely and which left its stamp, as was only to be expected, on my impressionable years, those which govern the fabrication of character, I refer to the period which extends, as far as the eye can see, from the first totterings, behind a chair, to the third form, in which I concluded my studies. I had then the deplorable habit, having pissed in my trousers, or shat there, which I did fairly regularly early in the morning, about ten or half past ten, of persisting in going on and finishing my day as if nothing had happened. The very idea of changing my trousers, or of confiding in mother, who goodness knows asked nothing better than to help me, was unbearable, I don't know why, and till bedtime I dragged on with burning and stinking between my little thighs, or sticking to my bottom, the result of my incontinence. Whence this wary way of walking, with legs stiff and wide apart, and this desperate rolling of the bust, no doubt intended to put people off the scent, to make them think I was full of gaiety and high spirits, without a care in the world, and to lend plausibility to my explanations concerning my nether rigidity, which I ascribed to hereditary rheumatism. My youthful ardour, in so far as I had any, spent itself in this effort, I became sour and mistrustful, a little before my time, in love with hiding and the prone position. Poor juvenile solutions, explaining nothing. No need then for caution, we may reason on to our heart's content, the fog won't lift.

The weather was fine. I advanced down the street, keeping as close as I could to the sidewalk. The widest sidewalk is never wide enough for me, once I set myself in motion, and I hate to

7

inconvenience strangers. A policeman stopped me and said, The street for vehicles, the sidewalk for pedestrians. Like a bit of Old Testament. So I got back on the sidewalk, almost apologetically, and persevered there, in spite of an indescribable jostle, for a good twenty steps, till I had to fling myself to the ground to avoid crushing a child. He was wearing a little harness, I remember, with little bells, he must have taken himself for a pony, or a Clydesdale, why not. I would have crushed him gladly, I loathe children, and it would have been doing him a service, but I was afraid of reprisals. Everyone is a parent, that is what keeps you from hoping. One should reserve, on busy streets, special tracks for these nasty little creatures, their prams, hoops, sweets, scooters, skates, grandpas, grandmas, nannies, balloons and balls, all their foul little happiness in a word. I fell then, and brought down with me an old lady covered with spangles and lace who must have weighed about sixteen stone. Her screams soon drew a crowd. I had high hopes she had broken her femur, old ladies break their femur easily, but not enough, not enough. I took advantage of the confusion to make off, muttering unintelligible oaths, as if I were the victim, and I was, but I couldn't have proved it. They never lynch children, babies, no matter what they do they are whitewashed in advance. I personally would lynch them with the utmost pleasure, I don't say I'd lend a hand, no, I am not a violent man, but I'd encourage the others and stand them drinks when it was done. But no sooner had I begun to reel on than I was stopped by a second policeman, similar in all respects to the first, so much so that I wondered whether it was not the same one. He pointed out to me that the sidewalk was for everyone, as if it was quite obvious that I could not be assimilated to that category. Would you like me, I said, without thinking for a single moment of Heraclitus, to get down in the gutter? Get down wherever you want, he said, but leave some room for others. If you can't bloody well get about like everyone else, he said, you'd do better to stay at home. It was exactly my feeling. And that he should attribute to me a home was no small satisfaction. At that moment a funeral passed, as sometimes happens. There was a great flurry of hats and at the same time a flutter of countless fingers. Personally if I were reduced to making the sign of the cross I would set my heart on doing it right, nose, navel, left nipple, right nipple. But the way they did it, slovenly and wild, he seemed crucified all of a heap, no dignity, his knees under his chin and his hands anyhow. The more fervent stopped dead and muttered. As for the policeman he stiffened to attention, closed his eyes and saluted. Through the windows of the cabs I caught a glimpse of the mourners conversing with animation, no doubt scenes from the life of their late dear brother in Christ, or sister. I seem to have heard that the hearse trappings are not the same in both cases, but I never could find out what the difference consists in. The horses were farting and shitting as if they were going to the fair. I saw no one kneeling.

But with us the last journey is soon done, it is in vain you quicken your pace, the last cab containing the domestics soon leaves you behind, the respite is over, the bystanders go their ways, you may look to yourself again. So I stopped a third time, of my own free will, and entered a cab. Those I had just seen pass, crammed with people hotly arguing, must have made a strong impression on me. It's a big black box, rocking and swaying on its springs, the windows are small, you curl up in a corner, it smells musty. I felt my hat grazing the roof. A little later I leant forward and closed the windows. Then I sat down again with my back to the horse. I was dozing off when a voice made me start, the cabman's. He had opened the door, no doubt despairing of making himself heard through the window. All I saw was his moustache. Where to? he said. He had climbed down from his seat on purpose to ask me that. And I who thought I was far away already. I reflected, searching in my memory for the name of a street, or a monument. Is your cab for sale? I said. I added, Without the horse. What could I do with a horse? But what would I do with a cab? Could I as much as stretch out in it? Who would bring me food? To the Zoo, I said. It is rare for a capital to be without a Zoo. I added, Don't go too fast. He laughed. The suggestion that he might go too fast to the Zoo must have amused him. Unless it was the prospect of being cabless. Unless it was simply myself, my own person, whose presence in the cab must have transformed it, so much so that the cabman, seeing me there with my head in the shadows of the roof and my knees against the window, had wondered perhaps if it was really his cab, really a cab. He hastens to look at his horse, and is reassured. But does one ever know oneself why one laughs? His laugh in any case was brief, which suggested I was not the joke. He closed the door and climbed back to his seat. It was not long then before the horse got under way.

Yes, surprising though it may seem, I still had a little money at this time. The small sum my father had left me as a gift, with no restrictions, at his death, I still wonder if it wasn't stolen from me. Then I had none. And yet my life went on, and even in the way I wanted, up to a point. The great disadvantage of this condition, which might be defined as the absolute impossibility of all purchase, is that it compels you to bestir yourself. It is rare, for example, when you are completely penniless, that you can have food brought to you from time to time in your retreat. You are therefore obliged to go out and bestir yourself, at least one day a week. You can hardly have a home address under these circumstances, it's inevitable. It was therefore with a certain delay that I learnt they were looking for me, for an affair concerning me. I forget through what channel. I did not read the newspapers, nor do I remember having spoken with anyone during these years, except perhaps three or four times, on the subject of food. At any rate, I must have had wind of the affair one way or another, otherwise I would never have gone to see the lawyer, Mr. Nidder, strange how one fails to forget certain names, and he would never have received me. He verified my identity. That took some time. I showed him the metal initials in the lining of my hat, they proved nothing but they increased the probabilities. Sign, he said. He played with a cylindrical ruler, you could have felled an ox with it. Count, he said. A young woman, perhaps venal, was present at this interview, as a witness no doubt. I stuffed the wad in my pocket. You shouldn't do that, he said. It occurred to me that he should have asked me to count before I signed, it would have been more in order. Where can I reach you, he said, if necessary? At the foot of the stairs I thought of something. Soon after I went back to ask him where this money came from, adding that I had a right to know. He gave me a woman's name that I've forgotten. Perhaps she had dandled me on her knees while I was still in swaddling clothes and there had been some lovey-dovey. Sometimes that suffices. I repeat, in swaddling clothes, for any later it would have been too late, for lovey-dovey. It is thanks to this money then that I still had a little. Very little. Divided by my life to come it was negligible, unless my conjectures were unduly pessimistic. I knocked on the partition beside my hat, right in the cabman's back if my calculations were correct. A cloud of dust rose from the upholstery. I took a stone from my pocket and knocked with the stone, until the cab stopped. I noticed that, unlike most vehicles, which slow down before stopping, the cab stopped dead. I waited. The whole cab shook. The cabman, on his high seat, must have been listening. I saw the horse as with my eyes of flesh. It had not lapsed into the drooping attitude of its briefest halts, it remained alert, its ears pricked up. I looked out of the window, we were again in motion. I banged again on the partition, until the cab stopped again. The cabman got down cursing from his seat. I lowered the window to prevent his opening the door. Faster, faster. He was redder than ever, purple in other words. Anger, or the rushing wind. I told him I was hiring him for the day. He replied that he had a funeral at three o'clock. Ah the dead. I told him I had changed my mind and no longer wished to go to the Zoo. Let us not go to the Zoo, I said. He replied that it made no difference to him where we went provided it wasn't too far, because of his beast. And they talk to us about the specificity of primitive people's speech. I asked him if he knew of an eating-house. I added, You'll eat with me. I prefer being with a regular customer in such places. There was a long table with two benches of exactly the same length on either side. Across the table he spoke to me of his life, of his wife, of his beast, then again of his life, of the atrocious life that was his, chiefly because of his character. He asked me if I realized what it meant to be out of doors in all weathers. I learnt there were still some cabmen who spent their day snug and warm inside their cabs on the rank, waiting for a customer to come and rouse them. Such a thing was possible in the past, but nowadays other methods were necessary, if a man was to have a little laid up at the end of his days. I described my situation to him, what I had lost and what I was looking for. We did our best, both of us, to understand, to explain. He understood that I had lost my room and needed another, but all the rest escaped him. He had taken it into his head, whence nothing could ever dislodge it, that I was looking for a furnished room. He took from his pocket an evening paper of the day before, or perhaps the day before that again, and proceeded to run through the advertisements, five or six of which he underlined with a tiny pencil, the same that hovered over the likely outsiders. He underlined no doubt those he would have underlined if he had been in my shoes, or perhaps those concentrated in the same area, because of his beast. I would only have confused him by saying that I could tolerate no furniture in my room except the bed, and that all the other pieces, and even the very night-table, had to be removed before I would consent to set foot in it. About three o'clock we roused the horse and set off again. The cabman suggested I climb up beside him on the seat, but for some time already I had been dreaming of the inside of the cab and I got back inside. We visited, methodically I hope, one after another, the addresses he had underlined. The short winter's day was drawing to a close. It seems to me sometimes that these are the only days I have ever known, and especially that most charming moment of all, just before night wipes them out. The addresses he had underlined, or rather marked with a cross, as common people do, proved fruitless one by one, and one by one he crossed them out with a diagonal stroke. Later he showed me the paper, advising me to keep it safe so as to be sure not to look again where I had already looked in vain. In spite of the closed windows, the creaking of the cab and the traffic noises, I heard him singing, all alone aloft on his seat. He had preferred me to a funeral, this was a fact which would endure forever. He sang, *She is far from the land where her young hero*, those are the only words I remember. At each stop he got down from his seat and helped me down from mine. I rang at the door he directed me to and sometimes I disappeared inside the house. It was a strange feeling, I remember, a house all about me again, after so long. He waited for me on the sidewalk and helped me climb back into the cab. I was sick and tired of this cabman. He clambered back to his seat and we set off again. At a certain moment there occurred this. He stopped. I shook off my torpor and made ready to get down. But he did not come to open the door and offer me his arm, so that I was obliged to get down by myself. He was lighting the lamps. I love oil lamps, in spite of their having been, with candles, and if I except the stars, the first lights I ever knew. I asked him if I might light the second lamp, since he had already lit the first himself. He gave me his box of matches, I swung open on its hinges the little convex glass, lit and closed at once, so that the wick might burn steady and bright, snug in its little house, sheltered from the wind. I had this joy. We saw nothing, by the light of these lamps, save the vague outlines of the horse, but the others saw them from afar, two yellow glows sailing slowly through the air. When the equipage turned an eye could be seen, red or green as the case might be, a bossy rhomb, as clear and keen as stained glass.

After we had verified the last address the cabman suggested bringing me to a hotel he knew where I would be comfortable. That makes sense, cabman, hotel, it's plausible. With his recommendation I would want for nothing. Every convenience, he said, with a wink. I place this conversation on the sidewalk, in front of the house from which I had just emerged. I remember, beneath the lamp, the flank of the horse, hollow and damp, and on the handle of the door the cabman's hand in its woollen glove. The roof of the cab was on a level with my neck. I suggested we have a drink. The horse had neither eaten nor drunk all day. I mentioned this to the cabman, who replied that his beast would take no food till it was back in the stable. If it ate anything whatever, during work, were it but an apple or a lump of sugar, it would have stomach pains and colics that would root it to the spot and might even kill it. That was why he was compelled to tie its jaws together with a strap whenever for one reason or another he had to let it out of his sight, so that it would not have to suffer from the kind hearts of the passers-by. After a few drinks the cabman invited me to do his wife and him the honour of spending the night in their home. It was not far. Recollecting these emotions, with the celebrated advantage of tranquillity, it seems to me he did nothing else, all that day, but turn about his lodging. They lived above a stable, at the back of a yard. Ideal location, I could have done with it. Having presented me to his wife, extraordinarily full-bottomed, he left us. She was manifestly ill at ease, alone with me. I could understand her, I don't stand on ceremony on these occasions. No reason for this to end or go on. Then let it end. I said I would go down to the stable and sleep there. The cabman protested. I insisted. He drew his wife's attention to the pustule on top of my skull, for I had removed my hat out of civility. He should have that removed, she said. The cabman named a doctor he held in high esteem who had rid him of an induration of the seat. If he wants to sleep in the stable, said his wife, let him sleep in the stable. The cabman took the lamp from the table and preceded me down the stairs, or rather ladder, which descended to the stable, leaving his wife in the dark. He spread a horse blanket on the ground in a corner on the straw and left me a box of matches in case I needed to see clearly in the night. I don't remember what the horse was doing all this time. Stretched out in the dark I heard the noise it made as it drank, a noise like no other, the sudden gallop of the rats and above me the muffled voices of the cabman and his wife as they criticized me. I held the box of matches in my hand, a big box of safety matches. I got up during the night and struck one. Its brief flame enabled me to locate the cab. I was seized, then abandoned, by the desire to set fire to the stable. I found the cab in the dark, opened the door, the rats poured out, I climbed in. As I settled down I noticed that the cab was no longer level, it was inevitable, with the shafts resting on the ground. It was better so, that allowed me to lie well back, with my feet higher than my head on the other seat. Several times during the night I felt the horse looking at me through the window and the breath of its nostrils. Now that it was unharnessed it must have been puzzled by my presence in the cab. I was cold, having forgotten to take the blanket, but not quite enough to go and get it. Through the window of the cab I saw the window of the stable, more and more clearly. I got out of the cab. It was not so dark now in the stable, I could make out the manger, the rack, the harness hanging, what else, buckets and brushes. I went to the door but couldn't open it. The horse didn't take its eyes off me. Don't horses ever sleep? It seemed to me the cabman should have tied it, to the manger for example. So I was obliged to leave by the window. It wasn't easy. But what is easy? I went out head first, my hands were flat on the ground of the yard while my legs were still thrashing to get clear of the frame. I remember the tufts of grass on which I pulled with both hands, in my effort to extricate myself. I should have taken off my greatcoat and thrown it through the window, but that would have meant thinking of it. No sooner had I left the yard than I thought of something. Weakness. I slipped a banknote in the matchbox, went back to the yard and placed the box on the sill of the window through which I had just come. The horse was at the window. But after I had taken a few steps in the street I returned to the yard and took back my banknote. I left the matches, they were not mine. The horse was still at the window. I was sick and tired of this cabhorse. Dawn was just breaking. I did not know where I was. I made towards the rising sun, towards where I thought it should rise, the quicker to come into the light. I would have liked a sea horizon, or a desert one. When I am abroad in the morning I go to meet the sun, and in the evening, when I am abroad, I follow it, till I am down among the dead. I don't know why I told this story. I could just as well have told another. Perhaps some other time I'll be able to tell another. Living souls, you will see how alike they are.

The Calmative

I don't know when I died. It always seemed to me I died old, about ninety years old, and what years, and that my body bore it out, from head to foot. But this evening, alone in my icy bed, I have the feeling I'll be older than the day, the night, when the sky with all its lights fell upon me, the same I had so often gazed on since my first stumblings on the distant earth. For I'm too frightened this evening to listen to myself rot, waiting for the great red lapses of the heart, the tearings at the caecal walls, and for the slow killings to finish in my skull, the assaults on unshakable pillars, the fornications with corpses. So I'll tell myself a story, I'll try and tell myself another story, to try and calm myself, and it's there I feel I'll be old, old, even older than the day I fell, calling for help, and it came. Or is it possible that in this story I have come back to life, after my death? No, it's not like me to come back to life, after my death.

What possessed me to stir when I wasn't with anybody? Was I being thrown out? No, I wasn't with anybody. I see a kind of den littered with empty tins. And yet we are not in the country. Perhaps it's just ruins, a ruined folly, on the skirts of the town, in a field, for the fields come right up to our walls, their walls, and the cows lie down at night in the lee of the ramparts. I have changed refuge so often, in the course of my rout, that now I can't tell between dens and ruins. But there was never any city but the one. It is true you often move along in a dream, houses and factories darken the air, trams go by and under your feet wet from the grass there are suddenly cobbles. I only know the city of my childhood, I must have seen the other, but unbelieving. All I say cancels out, I'll have said nothing. Was I hungry itself? Did the weather tempt me? It was cloudy and cool, I insist, but not to the extent of luring me out. I couldn't get up at the first attempt, nor let us say at the second, and once up, propped against the wall, I wondered if I could go on, I mean up, propped against the wall. Impossible to go out and walk. I speak as though it all happened yesterday. Yesterday indeed is recent, but not enough. For what I tell this evening is passing this evening, at this passing hour. I'm no longer with these assassins, in this bed of terror, but in my distant refuge, my hands twined together, my head bowed, weak, breathless, calm, free, and older than I'll have ever been, if my calculations are correct. I'll tell my story in the past none the less, as though it were a myth, or an old fable, for this evening I need another age, that age to become another age in which I became what I was.

But little by little I got myself out and started walking with short steps among the trees, oh look, trees! The paths of other days were rank with tangled growth. I leaned against the trunks to get my breath and pulled myself forward with the help of boughs. Of my last passage no trace remained. They were the perishing oaks immortalized by d'Aubigné. It was only a grove. The fringe was near, a light less green and kind of tattered told me so, in a whisper. Yes, no matter where you stood, in this little wood, and were it in the furthest recess of its poor secrecies, you saw on every hand the gleam of this pale light, promise of God knows what fatuous eternity. Die without too much pain, a little, that's worth your while. Under the blind sky close with your own hands the eyes soon sockets, then quick into carrion not to mislead the crows. That's the advantage of death by drowning, one of the advantages, the crabs never get there too soon. But here a strange thing, I was no sooner free of the wood at last, having crossed unminding the ditch that girdles it, than thoughts came to me of cruelty, the kind that smiles. A lush pasture lay before me, nonsuch perhaps, who cares, drenched in evening dew or recent rain. Beyond this meadow to my certain knowledge a path, then a field and finally the ramparts, closing the prospect. Cyclopean and crenellated, standing out faintly against a sky scarcely less sombre, they did not seem in ruins, viewed from mine, but were, to my certain knowledge. Such was the scene offered to me, in vain, for I knew it well and loathed it. What I saw was a bald man in a brown suit, a comedian. He was telling a funny story about a fiasco. Its point escaped me. He used the word snail, or slug, to the delight of all present. The women seemed even more entertained than their escorts, if that were possible. Their shrill laughter pierced the clapping and, when this had subsided, broke out still here and there in sudden peals even after the next story had begun, so that part of it was lost. Perhaps they had in mind the reigning penis sitting who knows by their side and from that sweet shore launched their cries of joy towards the comic vast, what a talent. But it's to me this evening something has to happen, to my body as in myth and metamorphosis, this old body to which nothing ever happened, or so little, which never met with anything, loved anything, wished for anything, in its tarnished universe, except for the mirrors to shatter, the plane, the curved, the magnifying, the minifying, and to vanish in the havoc of its images. Yes, this evening it has to be as in the story my father used to read to me, evening after evening, when I was small, and he had all his health, to calm me, evening after evening, year after year it seems to me this evening, which I don't remember much about, except that it was the adventures of one Joe Breem, or Breen, the son of a lighthouse-keeper, a strong muscular lad of fifteen, those were the words, who swam for miles in the night, a knife between his teeth, after a shark, I forget why, out of sheer heroism. He might have simply told me the story, he knew it by heart, so did I, but that wouldn't have calmed me, he had to read it to me, evening after evening, or pretend to read it to me, turning the pages and explaining the pictures that were of me already, evening after evening the same pictures till I dozed off on his shoulder. If he had skipped a single word I would have hit him, with my little fist, in his big belly bursting out of the old cardigan and unbuttoned trousers that rested him from his office canonicals. For me now the setting forth, the struggle and perhaps the return, for the old man I am this evening, older than my father ever was, older than

I shall ever be. I crossed the meadow with little stiff steps at the same time limp, the best I could manage. Of my last passage no trace remained, it was long ago. And the little bruised stems soon straighten up again, having need of air and light, and as for the broken their place is soon taken. I entered the town by what they call the Shepherds' Gate without having seen a soul, only the first bats like flying crucifixions, nor heard a sound except my steps, my heart in my breast and then, as I went under the arch, the hoot of an owl, that cry at once so soft and fierce which in the night, calling, answering, through my little wood and those nearby, sounded in my shelter like a tocsin. The further I went into the city the more I was struck by its deserted air. It was lit as usual, brighter than usual, although the shops were shut. But the lights were on in their windows with the object no doubt of attracting customers and prompting them to say, I say, I like that, not dear either, I'll come back tomorrow, if I'm still alive. I nearly said, Good God it's Sunday. The trams were running, the buses too, but few, slow, empty, noiseless, as if under water. I didn't see a single horse! I was wearing my long green greatcoat with the velvet collar, such as motorists wore about 1900, my father's, but that day it was sleeveless, a vast cloak. But on me it was still the same great dead weight, with no warmth to it, and the tails swept the ground, scraped it rather, they had grown so stiff, and I so shrunken. What would, what could happen to me in this empty place? But I felt the houses packed with people, lurking behind the curtains they looked out into the street or, crouched far back in the depths of the room, head in hands, were sunk in dream. Up aloft my hat, the same as always, I reached no further. I went right across the city and came to the sea, having followed the river to its mouth. I kept saying, I'll go back, unbelieving. The boats at anchor in the harbour, tied up to the jetty, seemed no less numerous than usual, as if I knew anything about what was usual. But the quays were deserted and there was no sign or stir of arrival or departure. But all might change from one moment to the next and be transformed like magic before my eyes. Then all the bustle of

the people and things of the sea, the masts of the big craft
gravely rocking and the small more jauntily, I insist, and I'd hear
the gulls' terrible cry and perhaps the sailors' cry. And I might
slip unnoticed aboard a freighter outward bound and get far
away and spend far away a few good months, perhaps a year or
two, in the sun, in peace, before I died. And without going that
far it would be a sad state of affairs if in that unscandalizable
throng I couldn't achieve a little encounter that would calm
me a little, or exchange a few words with a navigator for
example, words to carry away with me to my refuge, to add to
my collection. I waited sitting on a kind of topless capstan,
saying, The very capstans this evening are out of order. And I
gazed out to sea, out beyond the breakwaters, without sighting
the least vessel. I could see lights flush with the water. And the
pretty beacons at the harbour mouth I could see too, and others
in the distance, flashing from the coast, the islands, the head-
lands. But seeing still no sign or stir I made ready to go, to turn
away sadly from this dead haven, for there are scenes that
call for strange farewells. I had merely to bow my head and
look down at my feet, for it is in this attitude I always drew the
strength to, how shall I say, I don't know, and it was always from
the earth, rather than from the sky, notwithstanding its reputation, that my help came in time of trouble. And there, on the
flagstone, which I was not focusing, for why focus it, I saw haven
afar, where the black swell was most perilous, and all about me
storm and wreck. I'll never come back here, I said. But when
with a thrust of both hands against the rim of the capstan I
heaved myself up I found facing me a young boy holding a goat
by a horn. I sat down again. He stood there silent looking at me
without visible fear or revulsion. Admittedly the light was poor.
His silence seemed natural to me, it befitted me as the elder to
speak first. He was barefoot and in rags. Haunter of the water-
front he had stepped aside to see what the dark hulk could be
abandoned on the quayside. Such was my train of thought.
Close up to me now with his little guttersnipe's eye there could
be no doubt left in his mind. And yet he stayed. Can this base

thought be mine? Moved, for after all that is what I must have come out for, in a way, and with little expectation of advantage from what might follow, I resolved to speak to him. So I marshalled the words and opened my mouth, thinking I would hear them. But all I heard was a kind of rattle, unintelligible even to me who knew what was intended. But it was nothing, mere speechlessness due to long silence, as in the wood that darkens the mouth of hell, do you remember, I only just. Without letting go of his goat he moved right up against me and offered me a sweet out of a twist of paper such as you could buy for a penny. I hadn't been offered a sweet for eighty years at least, but I took it eagerly and put it in my mouth, the old gesture came back to me, more and more moved since that is what I wanted. The sweets were stuck together and I had my work cut out to separate the top one, a green one, from the others, but he helped me and his hand brushed mine. And a moment later as he made to move away, hauling his goat after him, with a great gesticulation of my whole body I motioned him to stay and I said, in an impetuous murmur, Where are you off to, my little man, with your nanny? The words were hardly out of my mouth when for shame I covered my face. And yet they were the same I had tried to utter but a moment before. Where are you off to, my little man, with your nanny! If I could have blushed I would have, but there was not enough blood left in my extremities. If I had had a penny in my pocket I would have given it to him, for him to forgive me, but I did not have a penny in my pocket, nor anything resembling it. Nothing that could give pleasure to a little unfortunate at the mouth of life. I suspect I had nothing with me but my stone, that day, having gone out as it were without premeditation. Of his little person I was fated to see no more than the black curly hair and the pretty curve of the long bare legs all muscle and dirt. And the hand, so fresh and keen, I would not forget in a hurry either. I looked for better words to say to him, I found them too late, he was gone, oh not far, but far. Out of my life too he went without a care, not one of his thoughts would ever be for me again, unless perhaps when he was old and, delving in his boyhood, would come upon that gallows night and hold the goat by the horn again and linger again a moment by my side, with who knows perhaps a touch of tenderness, even of envy, but I have my doubts. Poor dear dumb beasts, how you will have helped me. What does your daddy do? that's what I would have said to him if he had given me the chance. Soon they were no more than a single blur which if I hadn't known I might have taken for a young centaur. I was nearly going to have the goat dung, then pick up a handful of the pellets so soon cold and hard, sniff and even taste them, no, that would not help me this evening. I say this evening as if it were always the same evening, but are there two evenings? I went, intending to get back as fast as I could, but it would not be quite empty-handed, repeating, I'll never come back here. My legs were paining me, every step would gladly have been the last, but the glances I darted towards the windows, stealthily, showed me a great cylinder sweeping past as though on rollers on the asphalt. I must indeed have been moving fast, for I overhauled more than one pedestrian, there are the first men, without extending myself, I who in the normal way was left standing by cripples, and then I seemed to hear the footfalls die behind me. And yet each little step would gladly have been the last. So much so that when I emerged on a square I hadn't noticed on the way out, with a cathedral looming on the far side, I decided to go in, if it was open, and hide, as in the Middle Ages, for a space. I say cathedral, it may not have been, I don't know, all I know is it would vex me in this story that aspires to be the last, to have taken refuge in a common church. I remarked the Saxon Stützenwechsel. Charming effect, but it didn't charm me. The brilliantly lit nave appeared deserted. I walked round it several times without seeing a soul. They were hiding perhaps, under the choir-stalls, or dodging behind the pillars, like woodpeckers. Suddenly close to where I was, and without my having heard the long preliminary rumblings, the organ began to boom. I sprang up from the mat on which I lay before the altar and hastened to the far end of the nave as if on my way out. But it was a side aisle and the door I disappeared through was not the exit. For instead of being restored to the night I found myself at the foot of a spiral staircase which I began to climb at top speed, mindless of my heart, like one hotly pursued by a homicidal maniac. This staircase faintly lit by I know not what means, slits perhaps, I mounted panting as far as the projecting gallery in which it culminated and which, separated from the void by a cynical parapet, encompassed a smooth round wall capped by a little dome covered with lead or verdigrised copper, phew, if that's not clear. People must have come here for the view, those who fall die on the way. Flattening myself against the wall I started round, clockwise. But I had hardly gone a few steps when I met a man revolving in the other direction, with the utmost circumspection. How I'd love to push him, or him to push me, over the edge. He gazed at me wild-eyed for a moment and then, not daring to pass me on the parapet side and surmising correctly that I would not relinquish the wall just to oblige him, abruptly turned his back on me, his head rather, for his back remained glued to the wall, and went back the way he had come so that soon there was nothing left of him but a left hand. It lingered a moment, then slid out of sight. All that remained to me was the vision of two burning eyes starting out of their sockets under a check cap. Into what nightmare thingness am I fallen? My hat flew off, but did not get far thanks to the string. I turned my head towards the staircase and lent an eye. Nothing. Then a little girl came into view followed by a man holding her by the hand, both pressed against the wall. He pushed her into the stairway, disappeared after her, turned and raised towards me a face that made me recoil. I could only see his bare head above the top step. When they were gone I called. I completed in haste the round of the gallery. No one. I saw on the horizon, where sky, sea, plain and mountain meet, a few low stars, not to be confused with the fires men light, at night, or that go alight alone. Enough. Back in the street I tried to find my way in the sky, where I knew the Bears so well. If I had seen someone I would have stopped him to ask, the most ferocious aspect would not have daunted me. I would have said, touching my hat, Pardon me your honour, the Shepherds' Gate for the love of God. I thought I could go no further, but no sooner had the impetus reached my legs than on I went, believe it or not, at a very fair pace. I wasn't returning empty-handed, not quite, I was taking back with me the virtual certainty that I was still of this world, of that world too, in a way. But I was paying the price. I would have done better to spend the night in the cathedral, on the mat before the altar, I would have continued on my way at first light, or they would have found me stretched out in the rigor of death, the genuine bodily article, under the blue eyes fount of so much hope, and put me in the evening papers. But suddenly I was descending a wide street, vaguely familiar, but in which I could never have set foot, in my lifetime. But soon realizing I was going downhill I turned about and set off in the other direction. For I was afraid if I went downhill of returning to the sea where I had sworn never to return. When I say I turned about I mean I wheeled round in a wide semicircle without slowing down, for I was afraid if I stopped of not being able to start again, yes, I was afraid of that too. And this evening too I dare not stop. I was struck more and more by the contrast between the brightly lit streets and their deserted air. To say it distressed me, no, but I say it all the same, in the hope of calming myself. To say there was no one abroad, no, I would not go that far, for I remarked a number of shapes, male and female, strange shapes, but not more so than usual. As to what hour it might have been I had no idea, except that it must have been some hour of the night. But it might have been three or four in the morning just as it might have been ten or eleven in the evening, depending no doubt on whether one wondered at the scarcity of passers-by or at the extraordinary radiance shed by the street-lamps and traffic-lights. For at one or other of these no one could fail to wonder, unless he was out of his mind. Not a single private car, but admittedly from time to time a public vehicle, slow sweep of light silent and empty. It is not my wish to labour these antinomies, for we are needless to say in a skull, but I have no choice but to add the following few remarks. All the mortals I saw were alone and as if sunk in themselves. It must be a common sight, but mixed with something else I imagine. The only couple was two men grappling, their legs intertwined. I only saw one cyclist! He was going the same way as I was. All were going the same way as I was, vehicles too, I have only just realized it. He was pedalling slowly in the middle of the street, reading a newspaper which he held with both hands spread open before his eyes. Every now and then he rang his bell without interrupting his reading. I watched him recede till he was no more than a dot on the horizon. Suddenly a young woman perhaps of easy virtue, dishevelled and her dress in disarray, darted across the street like a rabbit. That is all I had to add. But here a strange thing, yet another, I had no pain whatever, not even in my legs. Weakness. A good night's nightmare and a tin of sardines would restore my sensitivity. My shadow, one of my shadows, flew before me, dwindled, slid under my feet, trailed behind me the way shadows will. This degree of opacity appeared to me conclusive. But suddenly ahead of me a man on the same side of the street and going the same way, to keep harping on the same thing lest I forget. The distance between us was considerable, seventy paces at least, and fearing he might escape me I quickened my step with the result I swept forward as if on rollers. This is not me, I said, let us make the most of it. Finding myself in an instant a bare ten paces in his rear I slowed down so as not to burst in on him and so heighten the aversion my person inspired even in its most abject and obsequious attitudes. And a moment later, keeping humbly in step with him, Excuse me your honour, the Shepherds' Gate for the love of God! At close quarters he appeared normal apart from that air already noted of ebbing inward. I drew a few steps ahead, turned, cringed, touched my hat and said, The right time for mercy's sake! I might as well not have existed. But what about the sweet? A light! I cried. Given my need of help I can't think why I did not bar his path. I couldn't have, that's all, I couldn't have touched him. Seeing a stone seat by the kerb I sat down and crossed my legs, like Walther. I must have dozed off, for the next thing was a man sitting beside me. I was still taking him in when he opened his eyes and set them on me, as if for the first time, for he shrank back unaffectedly. Where did you spring from? he said. To hear myself addressed again so soon impressed me greatly. What's the matter with you? he said. I tried to look like one with whom that only is the matter which is native to him. Forgive me your honour, I said, gingerly lifting my hat and rising a fraction from the seat, the right time for the love of God! He said a time, I don't remember which, a time that explained nothing, that's all I remember, and did not calm me. But what time could have done that? Oh I know, I know, one will come that will. But in the meantime? What's that you said? he said. Unfortunately I had said nothing. But I wriggled out of it by asking him if he could help me find my way which I had lost. No, he said, for I am not from these parts and if I am sitting on this slab it is because the hotels were full or would not let me in, I have no opinion. But tell me the story of your life, then we'll see. My life! I cried. Why yes, he said, you know, that kind of—what shall I say? He brooded for a time, no doubt trying to think of what life could well be said to be a kind. In the end he went on, testily, Come now, everyone knows that. He jogged me in the ribs. No details, he said, the main drift, the main drift. But as I remained silent he said, Shall I tell you mine, then you'll see what I mean. The account he then gave was brief and dense, facts, without comment. That's what I call a life, he said, do you follow me now? It wasn't bad, his story, positively fairy-like in places. But that Pauline, I said, are you still with her? I am, he said, but I'm going to leave her and set up with another, younger and plumper. You travel a lot, I said. Oh widely, widely, he said. Words were coming back to me and the way to make them sound. All that's a thing of the past for you no doubt, he said. Do you think of spending some time among us? I said. This sentence struck me as particularly well turned. If it's not a rude question, he said, how old are you?

I don't know, I said. You don't know! he cried. Not exactly, I said. Are thighs much in your thoughts, he said, arses, cunts and environs? I didn't follow. No more erections naturally, he said. Erections? I said. The penis, he said, you know what the penis is, there, between the legs. Ah that! I said. It thickens, lengthens, stiffens and rises, he said, does it not? I assented, though they were not the terms I would have used. That is what we call an erection, he said. He pondered, then exclaimed, Phenomenal! No? Strange right enough, I said. And there you have it all, he said. But what will become of her? I said. Who? he said. Pauline, I said. She will grow old, he said with tranquil assurance, slowly at first, then faster and faster, in pain and bitterness, pulling the devil by the tail. The face was not full, but I eyed it in vain, it remained clothed in its flesh instead of turning all chalky and channelled as with a gouge. The very vomer kept its cushion. It is true discussion was always bad for me. I longed for the tender nonsuch, I would have trodden it gently, with my boots in my hand, and for the shade of my wood, far from this terrible light. What are you grinning and bearing? he said. He held on his knees a big black bag, like a midwife's I imagine. It was full of glittering phials. I asked him if they were all alike. Oho no, he said, for every taste. He took one and held it out to me, saying, One and six. What did he want? To sell it to me? Proceeding on this hypothesis I told him I had no money. No money! he cried. All of a sudden his hand came down on the back of my neck, his sinewy fingers closed and with a jerk and a twist he had me up against him. But instead of dispatching me he began to murmur words so sweet that I went limp and my head fell forward in his lap. Between the caressing voice and the fingers rowelling my neck the contrast was striking. But gradually the two things merged in a devastating hope, if I dare say so, and I dare. For this evening I have nothing to lose that I can discern. And if I have reached this point (in my story) without anything having changed, for if anything had changed I think I'd know, the fact remains I have reached it, and that's something, and with nothing changed, and that's something too. It's no excuse for rushing matters. No, it must cease gently, as gently cease on the stairs the steps of the loved one, who could not love and will not come back, and whose steps say so, that she could not love and will not come back. He suddenly shoved me away and showed me the phial again. There you have it all, he said. It can't have been the same all as before. Want it? he said. No, but I said yes, so as not to vex him. He proposed an exchange. Give me your hat, he said. I refused. What vehemence! he said. I haven't a thing, I said. Try in your pockets, he said. I haven't a thing, I said, I came out without a thing. Give me a lace, he said. I refused. Long silence. And if you gave me a kiss, he said finally. I knew there were kisses in the air. Can you take off your hat? he said. I took it off. Put it back, he said, you look nicer with it on. I put it back. Come on, he said, give me a kiss and let there be an end to it. Did it not occur to him I might turn him down? No, a kiss is not a bootlace, he must have seen from my face that all passion was not quite spent. Come, he said. I wiped my mouth in its tod of hair and advanced it towards his. Just a moment, he said. My mouth stood still. You know what a kiss is? he said. Yes yes, I said. If it's not a rude question, he said, when was your last? Some time ago, I said, but I can still do them. He took off his hat, a bowler, and tapped the middle of his forehead. There, he said, and there only. He had a noble brow, white and high. He leaned forward, closing his eyes. Quick, he said. I pursed up my lips as mother had taught me and brought them down where he had said. Enough, he said. He raised his hand to the spot, but left the gesture unfinished and put on his hat. I turned away and looked across the street. It was then I noticed we were sitting opposite a horse-butcher's. Here, he said, take it. I had forgotten. He rose. Standing he was quite short. One good turn, he said, with radiant smile. His teeth shone. I listened to his steps die away. How tell what remains? But it's the end. Or have I been dreaming, am I dreaming? No no, none of that, for dream is nothing, a joke, and significant what is worse. I said, Stay where you are till day breaks, wait sleeping till the lamps go out and the streets come to life. But I stood up and moved off. My pains were back, but with something untoward which prevented my wrapping them around me. But I said, Little by little you are coming to. From my gait alone, slow, stiff and which seemed at every step to solve a stato-dynamic problem never posed before, I would have been known again, if I had been known. I crossed over and stopped before the butcher's. Behind the grille the curtains were drawn, rough canvas curtains striped blue and white, colours of the Virgin, and stained with great pink stains. They did not quite meet in the middle and through the chink I could make out the dim carcasses of the gutted horses hanging from hooks head downwards. I hugged the walls, famished for shadow. To think that in a moment all will be said, all to do again. And the city clocks, what was wrong with them, whose great chill clang even in my wood fell on me from the air? What else? Ah yes, my spoils. I tried to think of Pauline, but she eluded me, gleamed an instant and was gone, like the young woman in the street. So I went in the atrocious brightness, bedded in my old flesh, straining towards an issue and passing them by to left and right and my mind panting after this and that and always flung back to where there was nothing. I succeeded however in fastening briefly on the little girl, long enough to see her a little more clearly than before, so that she wore a kind of bonnet and clasped in her hand a book, of common prayer perhaps, and to try and have her smile, but she did not smile, but vanished down the staircase without having yielded me her little face. I had to stop. At first nothing, then little by little, I mean rising up out of the silence till suddenly no higher, a kind of massive murmur coming perhaps from the house that was propping me up. That reminded me that the houses were full of people, besieged, no, I don't know. When I stepped back to look at the windows I could see, in spite of shutters, blinds and muslins, that many of the rooms were lit. The light was so dimmed by the brilliancy flooding the boulevard that short of knowing or suspecting it was not so one might have supposed everyone sleeping. The sound was not continuous, but broken by silences possibly of consternation. I thought of ringing at the door and asking for shelter and protection till morning. But suddenly I was on my way again. But little by little, in a slow swoon, darkness fell about me. I saw a mass of bright flowers fade in an exquisite cascade of paling colours. I found myself admiring, all along the housefronts, the gradual blossoming of squares and rectangles, casement and sash, yellow, green, pink, according to the curtains and blinds, finding that pretty. Then at last, before I fell, first to my knees, as cattle do, then on my face, I was in a throng. I didn't lose consciousness, when I lose consciousness it will not be to recover it. They paid no heed to me, though careful not to walk on me, a courtesy that must have touched me, it was what I had come out for. It was well with me, sated with dark and calm, lying at the feet of mortals, fathom deep in the grey of dawn, if it was dawn. But reality, too tired to look for the right word, was soon restored, the throng fell away, the light came back and I had no need to raise my head from the ground to know I was back in the same blinding void as before. I said, Stay where you are, down on the friendly stone, or at least indifferent, don't open your eyes, wait for morning. But up with me again and back on the way that was not mine, on uphill along the boulevard. A blessing he was not waiting for me, poor old Breem, or Breen. I said, The sea is east, it's west I must go, to the left of north. But in vain I raised without hope my eyes to the sky to look for the Bears. For the light I steeped in put out the stars, assuming they were there, which I doubted, remembering the clouds.

The End

They clothed me and gave me money. I knew what the money was for, it was to get me started. When it was gone I would have to get more, if I wanted to go on. The same for the shoes, when they were worn out I would have to get them mended, or get myself another pair, or go on barefoot, if I wanted to go on. The same for the coat and trousers, needless to say, with this difference, that I could go on in my shirtsleeves, if I wanted. The clothes—shoes, socks, trousers, shirt, coat, hat—were not new, but the deceased must have been about my size. That is to say, he must have been a little shorter, a little thinner, for the clothes did not fit me so well in the beginning as they did at the end, the shirt especially, and it was many a long day before I could button it at the neck, or profit by the collar that went with it, or pin the tails together between my legs in the way my mother had taught me. He must have put on his Sunday best to go to the consultation, perhaps for the first time, unable to bear it any longer. Be that as it may the hat was a bowler, in good shape. I said, Keep your hat and give me back mine. I added, Give me back my greatcoat. They replied that they had burnt them, together with my other clothes. I understood then that the end was near, at least fairly near. Later on I tried to exchange this hat for a cap, or a slouch which could be pulled down over my face, but without much success. And yet I could not go about bare-headed, with my skull in the state it was. At first this hat was too small, then it got used to me. They gave me a tie, after long discussion. It seemed a pretty tie to me, but I didn't like it. When it came at last I was too tired to send it back. But in the end it came in useful. It was blue, with kinds of little stars. I didn't feel well, but they told me I was well enough. They didn't say in so many words that I was as well as I would ever be, but that was the implication. I lay inert on the bed and it took three women to put on my trousers. They didn't seem to take much interest in my private parts which to tell the truth were nothing to write home about, I didn't take much interest in them myself. But they might have passed some remark. When they had finished I got up and finished dressing unaided. They told me to sit on the bed and wait. All the bedding had disappeared. It made me angry that they had not let me wait in the familiar bed, instead of leaving me standing in the cold, in these clothes that smelt of sulphur. I said, You might have left me in the bed till the last moment. Men all in white came in with mallets in their hands. They dismantled the bed and took away the pieces. One of the women followed them out and came back with a chair which she set before me. I had done well to pretend I was angry. But to make it quite clear to them how angry I was that they had not left me in my bed I gave the chair a kick that sent it flying. A man came in and made a sign to me to follow him. In the hall he gave me a paper to sign. What's this, I said, a safe-conduct? It's a receipt, he said, for the clothes and money you have received. What money? I said. It was then I received the money. To think I had almost departed without a penny in my pocket. The sum was not large, compared to other sums, but to me it seemed large. I saw the familar objects, companions of so many bearable hours. The stool, for example, dearest of all. The long afternoons together, waiting for it to be time for bed. At times I felt its wooden life invade me, till I myself became a piece of old wood. There was even a hole for my cyst. Then the window pane with the patch of frosting gone, where I used to press my eye in the hour of need, and rarely in vain. I am greatly obliged to you, I said, is there a law which prevents you from throwing me out naked and penniless? That would damage our reputation in the long run, he replied. Could they not possibly keep me a little longer, I said, I could make myself useful. Useful, he said, joking apart you would be willing to make yourself useful? A moment later he went on, If they believed you were really willing to make yourself useful they would keep you, I am sure. The number of times I had said I was going to make myself useful, I wasn't going to start that again. How weak I felt! Perhaps, I said, they would consent to take back the money and keep me a little longer. This is a charitable institution, he said, and the money is a gift you receive when you leave. When it is gone you will have to get more, if you want to go on. Never come back here whatever you do, you would not be let in. Don't go to any of our branches either, they would turn you away. Exelmans! I cried. Come come, he said, and anyway no one understands a tenth of what you say. I'm so old, I said. You are not so old as all that, he said. May I stay here just a little longer, I said, till the rain is over? You may wait in the cloister, he said, the rain will go on all day. You may wait in the cloister till six o'clock, you will hear the bell. If anyone challenges you, you need only say you have permission to shelter in the cloister. Whose name will I give? I said. Weir, he said.

I had not been long in the cloister when the rain stopped and the sun came out. It was low and I reckoned it must be getting on for six, considering the season. I stayed there looking through the archway at the sun as it went down behind the cloister. A man appeared and asked me what I was doing. What do you want? were the words he used. Very friendly. I replied that I had Mr. Weir's permission to stay in the cloister till six o'clock. He went away, but came back immediately. He must have spoken to Mr. Weir in the interim, for he said, You must not loiter in the cloister now the rain is over.

Now I was making my way through the garden. There was that strange light which follows a day of persistent rain, when the sun comes out and the sky clears too late to be of any use. The earth makes a sound as of sighs and the last drops fall from the emptied cloudless sky. A small boy, stretching out his hands and looking up at the blue sky, asked his mother how such a thing was possible. Fuck off, she said. I suddenly remembered I had not thought of asking Mr. Weir for a piece of bread. He would surely have given it to me. I had as a matter of fact thought of it during our conversation in the hall, I had said to myself, Let us first finish our conversation, then I'll ask.

I knew well they would not keep me. I would gladly have turned back, but I was afraid one of the guards would stop me and tell me I would never see Mr. Weir again. That might have added to my sorrow. And anyway I never turned back on such occasions.

In the street I was lost. I had not set foot in this part of the city for a long time and it seemed greatly changed. Whole buildings had disappeared, the palings had changed position and on all sides I saw, in great letters, the names of tradesmen I had never seen before and would have been at a loss to pronounce. There were streets where I remembered none, some I did remember had vanished and others had completely changed their names. The general impression was the same as before. It is true I did not know the city very well. Perhaps it was quite a different one. I did not know where I was supposed to be going. I had the great good fortune, more than once, not to be run over. My appearance still made people laugh, with that hearty jovial laugh so good for the health. By keeping the red part of the sky as much as possible on my right hand I came at last to the river. Here all seemed at first sight more or less as I had left it. But if I had looked more closely I would doubtless have discovered many changes. And indeed I subsequently did so. But the general appearance of the river, flowing between its quays and under its bridges, had not changed. Yes, the river still gave the impression it was flowing in the wrong direction. That's all a pack of lies I feel. My bench was still there. It was shaped to fit the curves of the seated body. It stood beside a watering trough, gift of a Mrs. Maxwell to the city horses, according to the inscription. During the short time I rested there several horses took advantage of this monument. The iron shoes approached and the jingle of the harness. Then silence. That was the horse looking at me. Then the noise of pebbles and mud that horses make when drinking. Then the silence again. That was the horse looking at me again. Then the pebbles again. Then the silence again. Till the horse had finished drinking or the driver deemed it had drunk its fill. The horses were uneasy. Once, when the noise stopped, I turned and saw the horse looking at me. The driver too was looking at me. Mrs. Maxwell would have been pleased if she could have seen her trough rendering such services to the city horses. When it was night, after a tedious twilight, I took off my hat which was paining me. I longed to be under cover again, in an empty place, close and warm, with artificial light, an oil lamp for choice, with a pink shade for preference. From time to time someone would come to make sure I was all right and needed nothing. It was long since I had longed for anything and the effect on me was horrible.

In the days that followed I visited several lodgings, without much success. They usually slammed the door in my face, even when I showed my money and offered to pay a week in advance, or even two. It was in vain I put on my best manners, smiled and spoke distinctly, they slammed the door in my face before I could even finish my little speech. It was at this time I perfected a method of doffing my hat at once courteous and discreet, neither servile nor insolent. I slipped it smartly forward, held it a second poised in such a way that the person addressed could not see my skull, then slipped it back. To do that naturally, without creating an unfavourable impression, is no easy matter. When I deemed that to tip my hat would suffice, I naturally did no more than tip it. But to tip one's hat is no easy matter either. I subsequently solved this problem, always fundamental in time of adversity, by wearing a kepi and saluting in military fashion, no, that must be wrong, I don't know, I had my hat at the end. I never made the mistake of wearing medals. Some landladies were in such need of money that they let me in immediately and showed me the room. But I couldn't come to an agreement with any of them. Finally I found a basement. With this woman I came to an agreement at once. My oddities, that's the expression she used, did not alarm her. She nevertheless insisted on making the bed and cleaning the room once a week, instead of once a month as I requested. She told me that while she was cleaning, which would not take long, I could wait in the area. She added, with a great deal of feeling, that she would never put me out in bad weather. This woman was Greek, I think, or Turkish. She never spoke about herself. I somehow got the idea she was a widow or at least that her husband had left her. She had a strange accent. But so had I with my way of assimilating the vowels and omitting the consonants.

Now I didn't know where I was. I had a vague vision, not a real vision, I didn't see anything, of a big house five or six stories high, one of a block perhaps. It was dusk when I got there and I did not pay the same heed to my surroundings as I might have done if I had suspected they were to close about me. And by then I must have lost all hope. It is true that when I left this house it was a glorious day, but I never look back when leaving. I must have read somewhere, when I was small and still read, that it is better not to look back when leaving. And yet I sometimes did. But even without looking back it seems to me I should have seen something when leaving. But there it is. All I remember is my feet emerging from my shadow, one after the other. My shoes had stiffened and the sun brought out the cracks in the leather.

I was comfortable enough in this house, I must say. Apart from a few rats I was alone in the basement. The woman did her best to respect our agreement. About noon she brought me a big tray of food and took away the tray of the previous day. At the same time she brought me a clean chamber-pot. The chamber-pot had a large handle which she slipped over her arm so that both her hands were free to carry the tray. The rest of the day I saw no more of her except sometimes when she peeped in to make sure nothing had happened to me. Fortunately I did not need affection. From my bed I saw the feet coming and going on the sidewalk. Certain evenings, when the weather was fine and I felt equal to it, I fetched my chair into the area and sat looking up into the skirts of the women passing by. Once I sent for a crocus bulb and planted it in the dark area, in an old pot. It must have been coming up to spring, it was probably not the right time for it. I left the pot outside, attached to a string I passed through the window. In the evening, when the weather was fine, a little light crept up the wall. Then I sat down beside the window and pulled on the string to keep the pot in the light and warmth. That can't have been easy, I don't see how I managed it. It was probably not the right thing for it. I manured it as best I could and pissed on it when the weather was dry. It may not have been the right thing for it. It sprouted, but never any flowers, just a wilting stem and a few chlorotic leaves. I would have liked to have a yellow crocus, or a hyacinth, but there, it was not to be. She wanted to take it away, but I told her to leave it. She wanted to buy me another, but I told her I didn't want another. What lacerated me most was the din of the newspaper boys. They went pounding by every day at the same hours, their heels thudding on the sidewalk, crying the names of their papers and even the headlines. The house noises disturbed me less. A little girl, unless it was a little boy, sang every evening at the same hour, somewhere above me. For a long time I could not catch the words. But hearing them day after day I finally managed to catch a few. Strange words for a little girl, or a little boy. Was it a song in my head or did it merely come from without? It was a sort of lullaby, I believe. It often sent me to sleep, even me. Sometimes it was a little girl who came. She had long red hair hanging down in two braids. I didn't know who she was. She lingered awhile in the room, then went away without a word. One day I had a visit from a policeman. He said I had to be watched, without explaining why. Suspicious, that was it, he told me I was suspicious. I let him talk. He didn't dare arrest me. Or perhaps he had a kind heart. A priest too, one day I had a visit from a priest. I informed him I belonged to a branch of the reformed church. He asked me what kind of clergyman I would like to see. Yes, there's that about the reformed church, you're lost, it's unavoidable. Perhaps he had a kind heart. He told me to let him know if I needed a helping hand. A helping hand! He gave me his name and explained where I could reach him. I should have made a note of it.

One day the woman made me an offer. She said she was in urgent need of cash and that if I could pay her six months in advance she would reduce my rent by one fourth during that period, something of that kind. This had the advantage of saving six weeks'(?) rent and the disadvantage of almost exhausting my small capital. But could you call that a disadvantage? Wouldn't I stay on in any case till my last penny was gone, and even longer, till she put me out? I gave her the money and she gave me a receipt.

One morning, not long after this transaction, I was awakened by a man shaking my shoulder. It could not have been much past eleven. He requested me to get up and leave his house immediately. He was most correct, I must say. His surprise, he said, was no less than mine. It was his house. His property. The Turkish woman had left the day before. But I saw her last night, I said. You must be mistaken, he said, for she brought the keys to my office no later than yesterday afternoon. But I just paid her six months' rent in advance, I said. Get a refund, he said. But I don't even know her name, I said, let alone her address. You don't know her name? he said. He must have thought I was lying. I'm sick, I said, I can't leave like this, without any notice. You're not so sick as all that, he said. He offered to send for a taxi, even an ambulance if I preferred. He said he needed the room immediately for his pig which even as he spoke was catching cold in a cart before the door and no one to look after him but a stray urchin whom he had never set eyes on before and who was probably busy tormenting him. I asked if he couldn't let me have another place, any old corner where I could lie down long enough to recover from the shock and decide what to do. He said he could not. Don't think I'm being unkind, he added. I could live here with the pig, I said, I'd look after him. The long months of peace wiped out in an instant! Come now, come now, he said, get a grip on yourself, be a man, get up, that's enough. After all it was no concern of his. He had really been most patient. He must have visited the basement while I was sleeping.

I felt weak. Perhaps I was. I stumbled in the blinding light. A bus took me into the country. I sat down in a field in the sun.

But it seems to me that was much later. I stuck leaves under my hat, all the way round, to make a shade. The night was cold. I wandered for hours in the fields. At last I found a heap of dung. The next day I started back to the city. They made me get off three buses. I sat down by the roadside and dried my clothes in the sun. I enjoyed doing that. I said to myself, There's nothing more to be done now, not a thing, till they are dry. When they were dry I brushed them with a brush, I think a kind of curry-comb, that I found in a stable. Stables have always been my salvation. Then I went to the house and begged a glass of milk and a slice of bread and butter. They gave me everything except the butter. May I rest in the stable? I said. No, they said. I still stank, but with a stink that pleased me. I much preferred it to my own which moreover it prevented me from smelling, except a waft now and then. In the days that followed I took the necessary steps to recover my money. I don't know exactly what happened, whether I couldn't find the address, or whether there was no such address, or whether the Greek woman was unknown there. I ransacked my pockets for the receipt, to try and decipher the name. It wasn't there. Perhaps she had taken it back while I was sleeping. I don't know how long I wandered thus, resting now in one place, now in another, in the city and in the country. The city had suffered many changes. Nor was the country as I remembered it. The general effect was the same. One day I caught sight of my son. He was striding along with a briefcase under his arm. He took off his hat and bowed and I saw he was as bald as a coot. I was almost certain it was he. I turned round to gaze after him. He went bustling along on his duck feet, bowing and scraping and flourishing his hat left and right. The insufferable son of a bitch.

One day I met a man I had known in former times. He lived in a cave by the sea. He had an ass that grazed winter and summer, over the cliffs, or along the little tracks leading down to the sea. When the weather was very bad this ass came down to the cave of his own accord and sheltered there till the storm was past. So they had spent many a night huddled together, while the wind howled and the sea pounded on the shore. With the help of this ass he could deliver sand, sea-wrack and shells to the townsfolk, for their gardens. He couldn't carry much at a time, for the ass was old and small and the town was far. But in this way he earned a little money, enough to keep him in tobacco and matches and to buy a piece of bread from time to time. It was during one of these excursions that he met me, in the suburbs. He was delighted to see me, poor man. He begged me to go home with him and spend the night. Stay as long as you like, he said. What's wrong with your ass? I said. Don't mind him, he said, he doesn't know you. I reminded him that I wasn't in the habit of staying more than two or three minutes with anyone and that the sea did not agree with me. He seemed deeply grieved to hear it. So you won't come, he said. But to my amazement I got up on the ass and off we went, in the shade of the red chestnuts springing from the sidewalk. I held the ass by the mane, one hand in front of the other. The little boys jeered and threw stones, but their aim was poor, for they only hit me once, on the hat. A policeman stopped us and accused us of disturbing the peace. My friend replied that we were as nature had made us, the boys too were as nature had made them. It was inevitable, under these conditions, that the peace should be disturbed from time to time. Let us continue on our way, he said, and order will soon be restored throughout your beat. We followed the quiet, dustwhite inland roads with their hedges of hawthorn and fuchsia and their footpaths fringed with wild grass and daisies. Night fell. The ass carried me right to the mouth of the cave, for in the dark I could not have found my way down the path winding steeply to the sea. Then he climbed back to his pasture.

I don't know how long I stayed there. The cave was nicely arranged, I must say. I treated my crablice with salt water and seaweed, but a lot of nits must have survived. I put compresses of seaweed on my skull, which gave me great relief, but not for long. I lay in the cave and sometimes looked out at the horizon. I saw above me a vast trembling expanse without islands or promontories. It was here I found the phial in my pocket. It was not broken, for the glass was not real glass. I thought Mr. Weir had confiscated all my belongings. My host was out most of the time. He fed me on fish. It is easy for a man, a proper man, to live in a cave, far from everybody. He invited me to stay as long as I liked. If I preferred to be alone he would gladly prepare another cave for me further on. He would bring me food every day and drop in from time to time to make sure I was all right and needed nothing. He was kind. Unfortunately I did not need kindness. You wouldn't know of a lake dwelling? I said. I couldn't bear the sea, its splashing and heaving, its tides and general convulsiveness. The wind at least sometimes stops. My hands and feet felt as though they were full of ants. This kept me awake for hours on end. If I stayed here something awful would happen to me, I said, and a lot of good that would do me. You'd get drowned, he said. Yes, I said, or jump off the cliff. And to think I couldn't live anywhere else, he said, in my cabin in the mountains I was wretched. Your cabin in the mountains? I said. He repeated the story of his cabin in the mountains, I had forgotten it, it was as though I were hearing it for the first time. I asked him if he still had it. He replied he had not seen it since the day he fled from it, but that he believed it was still there, a little decayed no doubt. But when he urged me to take the key I refused, saying I had other plans. You will always find me here, he said, if you ever need me. Ah people. He gave me his knife.

What he called his cabin in the mountains was a sort of wooden shed. The door had been removed, for firewood, or for some other purpose. The glass had disappeared from the window. The roof had fallen in at several places. The interior was divided, by the remains of a partition, into two unequal parts. If there had been any furniture it was gone. The vilest acts had been committed on the ground and against the walls. The floor was strewn with excrements, both human and animal, with condoms and vomit. In a cowpad a heart had been traced, pierced by an arrow. And yet there was nothing to attract

ts. I noticed the remains of abandoned nosegays. They had
greedily gathered, carried for miles, then thrown away,
because they were cumbersome or already withered. This was
the dwelling to which I had been offered the key.

The scene was the familiar one of grandeur and desolation.

Nevertheless it was a roof over my head. I rested on a bed of
ferns, gathered at great labour with my own hands. One day I
couldn't get up. The cow saved me. Goaded by the icy mist she
came in search of shelter. It was probably not the first time.
She can't have seen me. I tried to suck her, without much
success. Her udder was covered with dung. I took off my hat
and, summoning all my energy, began to milk her into it. The
milk fell to the ground and was lost, but I said to myself, No
matter, it's free. She dragged me across the floor, stopping from
time to time only to kick me. I didn't know our cows too could
be so inhuman. She must have recently been milked. Clutching
the dug with one hand I kept my hat under it with the other. But
in the end she prevailed. For she dragged me across the threshold and out into the giant streaming ferns, where I was forced to
let go.

As I drank the milk I reproached myself with what I had
done. I could no longer count on this cow and she would warn
the others. More master of myself I might have made a friend of
her. She would have come every day, perhaps accompanied by
other cows. I might have learnt to make butter, even cheese. But
I said to myself, No, all is for the best.

Once on the road it was all downhill. Soon there were carts,
but they all refused to take me up. In other clothes, with another
face, they might have taken me up. I must have changed since
my expulsion from the basement. The face notably seemed to
have attained its climacteric. The humble, ingenuous smile
would no longer come, nor the expression of candid misery,
showing the stars and the distaff. I summoned them, but they
would not come. A mask of dirty old hairy leather, with two
holes and a slit, it was too far gone for the old trick of please
your honour and God reward you and pity upon me. It was

disastrous. What would I crawl with in future? I lay down on the side of the road and began to writhe each time I heard a cart approaching. That was so they would not think I was sleeping or resting. I tried to groan, Help! Help! But the tone that came out was that of polite conversation. My hour was not yet come and I could no longer groan. The last time I had cause to groan I had groaned as well as ever, and no heart within miles of me to melt. What was to become of me? I said to myself, I'll learn again. I lay down across the road at a narrow place, so that the carts could not pass without passing over my body, with one wheel at least, or two if there were four. But the day came when, looking round me, I was in the suburbs, and from there to the old haunts it was not far, beyond the stupid hope of rest or less pain.

So I covered the lower part of my face with a black rag and went and begged at a sunny corner. For it seemed to me my eyes were not completely spent, thanks perhaps to the dark glasses my tutor had given me. He had given me the *Ethics* of Geulincz. They were a man's glasses, I was a child. They found him dead, crumpled up in the water closet, his clothes in awful disorder, struck down by an infarctus. Ah what peace. The *Ethics* had his name (Ward) on the fly-leaf, the glasses had belonged to him. The bridge, at the time I am speaking of, was of brass wire, of the kind used to hang pictures and big mirrors, and two long black ribbons served as wings. I wound them round my ears and then down under my chin where I tied them together. The lenses had suffered, from rubbing in my pocket against each other and against the other objects there. I thought Mr. Weir had confiscated all my belongings. But I had no further need of these glasses and used them merely to soften the glare of the sun. I should never have mentioned them. The rag gave me a lot of trouble. I got it in the end from the lining of my greatcoat, no, I had no greatcoat now, of my coat then. The result was a grey rag rather than a black, perhaps even chequered, but I had to make do with it. Till afternoon I held my face raised towards the southern sky, then towards the western till night. The bowl gave me a lot of trouble. I couldn't use my hat because of my skull. As for holding out my hand, that was quite out of the question. So I got a tin and hung it from a button of my greatcoat, what's the matter with me, of my coat, at pubis level. It did not hang plumb, it leaned respectfully towards the passer-by, he had only to drop his mite. But that obliged him to come up close to me, he was in danger of touching me. In the end I got a bigger tin, a kind of big tin box, and I placed it on the side-walk at my feet. But people who give alms don't much care to toss them, there's something contemptuous about this gesture which is repugnant to sensitive natures. To say nothing of their having to aim. They are prepared to give, but not for their gift to go rolling under the passing feet or under the passing wheels, to be picked up perhaps by some undeserving person. So they don't give. There are those, to be sure, who stoop, but generally speaking people who give alms don't much care to stoop. What they like above all is to sight the wretch from afar, get ready their penny, drop it in their stride and hear the God bless you dying away in the distance. Personally I never said that, nor anything like it, I wasn't much of a believer, but I did make a noise with my mouth. In the end I got a kind of board or tray and tied it to my neck and waist. It jutted out just at the right height, pocket height, and its edge was far enough from my person for the coin to be bestowed without danger. Some days I strewed it with flowers, petals, buds and that herb which men call fleabane, I believe, in a word whatever I could find. I didn't go out of my way to look for them, but all the pretty things of this description that came my way were for the board. They must have thought I loved nature. Most of the time I looked up at the sky, but without focusing it, for why focus it? Most of the time it was a mixture of white, blue and grey, and then at evening all the evening colours. I felt it weighing softly on my face, I rubbed my face against it, one cheek after the other, turning my head from side to side. Now and then to rest my neck I dropped my head on my chest. Then I could see the board in the distance, a haze of many colours. I leaned against the wall, but without nonchalance, I shifted my weight from one foot to the other and my hands clutched the lapels of my coat. To beg with your hands in your pockets makes a bad impression. It irritates the workers, especially in winter. You should never wear gloves either. There were guttersnipes who swept away all I had earned, under cover of giving me a coin. It was to buy sweets. I unbuttoned my trousers discreetly to scratch myself. I scratched myself in an upward direction, with four nails. I pulled on the hairs, to get relief. It passed the time, time flew when I scratched myself. Real scratching is superior to masturbation, in my opinion. One can masturbate up to the age of seventy, and even beyond, but in the end it becomes a mere habit. Whereas to scratch myself properly I would have needed a dozen hands. I itched all over, on the privates, in the bush up to the navel, under the arms, in the arse, and then patches of eczema and psoriasis that I could set raging merely by thinking of them. It was in the arse I had the most pleasure, I stuck in my forefinger up to the knuckle. Later, if I had to shit, the pain was atrocious. But I hardly shat any more. Now and then a flying machine flew by, sluggishly it seemed to me. Often at the end of the day I discovered the legs of my trousers all wet. That must have been the dogs. I personally pissed very little. If by chance the need came on me a little squirt in my fly was enough to relieve it. Once at my post I did not leave it till nightfall. I had no appetite, God tempered the wind to me. After work I bought a bottle of milk and drank it in the evening in the shed. Better still, I got a little boy to buy it for me, always the same, they wouldn't serve me, I don't know why. I gave him a penny for his pains. One day I witnessed a strange scene. Normally I didn't see a great deal. I didn't hear a great deal either. I didn't pay attention. Strictly speaking I wasn't there. Strictly speaking I believe I've never been anywhere. But that day I must have come back. For some time past a sound had been scarifying me. I did not investigate the cause, for I said to myself, It's going to stop. But as it did not stop I had no choice but to find out the cause. It was a man perched on the roof of a car

and haranguing the passers-by. That at least was my interpreta-
tion. He was bellowing so loud that snatches of his discourse
reached my ears. Union . . . brothers . . . Marx . . . capital . . .
bread and butter . . . love. It was all Greek to me. The car was
drawn up against the kerb, just in front of me, I saw the orator
from behind. All of a sudden he turned and pointed at me, as at
an exhibit. Look at this down and out, he vociferated, this left-
over. If he doesn't go down on all fours, it's for fear of being
impounded. Old, lousy, rotten, ripe for the muckheap. And
there are a thousand like him, worse than him, ten thousand,
twenty thousand—. A voice, Thirty thousand. Every day you
pass them by, resumed the orator, and when you have backed
a winner you fling them a farthing. Do you ever think? The
voice, God forbid. A penny, resumed the orator, tuppence—.
The voice, thruppence. It never enters your head, resumed the
orator, that your charity is a crime, an incentive to slavery,
stultification and organized murder. Take a good look at this
living corpse. You may say it's his own fault. Ask him if it's his
own fault. The voice, Ask him yourself. Then he bent forward
and took me to task. I had perfected my board. It now consisted
of two boards hinged together, which enabled me, when my
work was done, to fold it and carry it under my arm. I liked
doing little odd jobs. So I took off the rag, pocketed the
few coins I had earned, untied the board, folded it and put it
under my arm. Do you hear me, you crucified bastard! cried
the orator. Then I went away, although it was still light. But
generally speaking it was a quiet corner, busy but not over-
crowded, thriving and well-frequented. He must have been a
religious fanatic, I could find no other explanation. Perhaps
he was an escaped lunatic. He had a nice face, a little on the
red side.

I did not work every day. I had practically no expenses. I even
managed to put a little aside, for my very last days. The days I
did not work I spent lying in the shed. The shed was on a private
estate, or what had once been a private estate, on the riverside.
This estate, the main entrance to which opened on a narrow,

dark and silent street, was enclosed with a wall, except of course on the river front, which marked its northern boundary for a distance of about thirty yards. From the last quays beyond the water the eyes rose to a confusion of low houses, wasteland, hoardings, chimneys, steeples and towers. A kind of parade ground was also to be seen, where soldiers played football all the year round. Only the ground floor windows—no, I can't. The estate seemed abandoned. The gates were locked and the paths overgrown with grass. Only the ground floor windows had shutters. The others were sometimes lit at night, faintly, now one, now another. At least that was my impression. Perhaps it was reflected light. In this shed, the day I adopted it, I found a boat, upside down. I righted it, chocked it up with stones and pieces of wood, took out the thwarts and made my bed inside. The rats had difficulty in getting at me, because of the bulge of the hull. And yet they longed to. Just think of it, living flesh, for in spite of everything I was still living flesh. I had lived too long among rats, in my chance dwellings, to share the dread they inspire in the vulgar. I even had a soft spot in my heart for them. They came with such confidence towards me, it seemed without the least repugnance. They made their toilet with catlike gestures. Toads at evening, motionless for hours, lap flies from the air. They like to squat where cover ends and open air begins, they favour thresholds. But I had to contend now with water rats, exceptionally lean and ferocious. So I made a kind of lid with stray boards. It's incredible the number of boards I've come across in my lifetime, I never needed a board but there it was, I had only to stoop and pick it up. I liked doing little odd jobs, no, not particularly, I didn't mind. It completely covered the boat, I'm referring again to the lid. I pushed it a little towards the stern, climbed into the boat by the bow, crawled to the stern, raised my feet and pushed the lid back towards the bow till it covered me completely. But what did my feet push against? They pushed against a crossbar I nailed to the lid for that purpose, I liked these little odd jobs. But it was better to climb into the boat by the stern and pull back the lid with my hands till it completely covered me, then push it forward in the same way when I wanted to get out. As holds for my hands I planted two spikes just where I needed them. These little odds and ends of carpentry, if I may so describe it, carried out with whatever tools and material I chanced to find, gave me a certain pleasure. I knew it would soon be the end, so I played the part, you know, the part of— how shall I say, I don't know. I was comfortable enough in this boat, I must say. The lid fitted so well I had to pierce a hole. It's no good closing your eyes, you must leave them open in the dark, that is my opinion. I am not speaking of sleep, I am speaking of what I believe is called waking. In any case, I slept very little at this period, I wasn't sleepy, or I was too sleepy, I don't know, or I was afraid, I don't know. Flat then on my back I saw nothing except, dimly, just above my head, through the tiny chinks, the grey light of the shed. To see nothing at all, no, that's too much. I heard faintly the cries of the gulls ravening about the mouth of the sewer near by. In a spew of yellow foam, if my memory serves me right, the filth gushed into the river and the slush of birds above screaming with hunger and fury. I heard the lapping of water against the slip and against the bank and the other sound, so different, of open wave, I heard it too. I too, when I moved, felt less boat than wave, or so it seemed to me, and my stillness was the stillness of eddies. That may seem impossible. The rain too, I often heard it, for it often rained. Sometimes a drop, falling through the roof of the shed, exploded on me. All that composed a rather liquid world. And then of course there was the voice of the wind or rather those, so various, of its playthings. But what does it amount to? Howling, soughing, moaning, sighing. What I would have liked was hammer strokes, bang bang bang, clanging in the desert. I let farts to be sure, but hardly ever a real crack, they oozed out with a sucking noise, melted in the mighty never. I don't know how long I stayed there. I was very snug in my box, I must say. It seemed to me I had grown more independent of recent years. That no one came any more, that no one could come any more to ask me if I was all right and needed nothing, distressed me then but little. I was all right, yes, quite so, and the fear of getting worse was less with me. As for my needs, they had dwindled as it were to my dimensions and become, if I may say so, of so exquisite a quality as to exclude all thought of succour. To know I had a being, however faint and false, outside of me, had once had the power to stir my heart. You become unsociable, it's inevitable. It's enough to make you wonder sometimes if you are on the right planet. Even the words desert you, it's as bad as that. Perhaps it's the moment when the vessels stop communicating, you know, the vessels. There you are still between the two murmurs, it must be the same old song as ever, but Christ you wouldn't think so. There were times when I wanted to push away the lid and get out of the boat and couldn't, I was so indolent and weak, so content deep down where I was. I felt them hard upon me, the icy, tumultuous streets, the terrifying faces, the noises that slash, pierce, claw, bruise. So I waited till the desire to shit, or even to piss, lent me wings. I did not want to dirty my nest! And yet it sometimes happened, and even more and more often. Arched and rigid I edged down my trousers and turned a little on my side, just enough to free the hole. To contrive a little kingdom, in the midst of the universal muck, then shit on it, ah that was me all over. The excrements were me too, I know, I know, but all the same. Enough, enough, the next thing I was having visions, I who never did, except sometimes in my sleep, who never had, real visions, I'd remember, except perhaps as a child, my myth will have it so. I knew they were visions because it was night and I was alone in my boat. What else could they have been? So I was in my boat and gliding on the waters. I didn't have to row, the ebb was carrying me out. Anyway I saw no oars, they must have taken them away. I had a board, the remains of a thwart perhaps, which I used when I came too close to the bank, or when a pier came bearing down on me or a barge at its moorings. There were stars in the sky, quite a few. I didn't know what the weather was doing, I was neither cold nor warm and all seemed calm. The banks receded more and more, it was inevitable, soon I saw them no more. The lights grew fainter and fewer as the river widened. There on the land men were sleeping, bodies were gathering strength for the toil and joys of the morrow. The boat was not gliding now, it was tossing, buffeted by the choppy waters of the bay. All seemed calm and yet foam was washing aboard. Now the sea air was all about me, I had no other shelter than the land, and what does it amount to, the shelter of the land, at such a time. I saw the beacons, four in all, including a lightship. I knew them well, even as a child I had known them well. It was evening, I was with my father on a height, he held my hand. I would have liked him to draw me close with a gesture of protective love, but his mind was on other things. He also taught me the names of the mountains. But to have done with these visions I also saw the lights of the buoys, the sea seemed full of them, red and green and to my surprise even yellow. And on the slopes of the mountain, now rearing its unbroken bulk behind the town, the fires turned from gold to red, from red to gold. I knew what it was, it was the gorse burning. How often I had set a match to it myself, as a child. And hours later, back in my home, before I climbed into bed, I watched from my high window the fires I had lit. That night then, all aglow with distant fires, on sea, on land and in the sky, I drifted with the currents and the tides. I noticed that my hat was tied, with a string I suppose, to my buttonhole. I got up from my seat in the stern and a great clanking was heard. That was the chain. One end was fastened to the bow and the other round my waist. I must have pierced a hole beforehand in the floor-boards, for there I was down on my knees prying out the plug with my knife. The hole was small and the water rose slowly. It would take a good half hour, everything included, barring accidents. Back now in the stern-sheets, my legs stretched out, my back well propped against the sack stuffed with grass I used as a cushion, I swallowed my calmative. The sea, the sky, the mountains and the islands closed in and crushed me in a mighty systole, then scattered to the uttermost confines of space. The memory came faint and cold of the story I might have told, a story in the likeness of my life, I mean without the courage to end or the strength to go on.

First Love

First Love

I associate, rightly or wrongly, my marriage with the death of my father, in time. That other links exist, on other levels, between these two affairs, is not impossible. I have enough trouble as it is in trying to say what I think I know.

I visited, not so long ago, my father's grave, that I do know, and noted the date of his death, of his death alone, for that of his birth had no interest for me, on that particular day. I set out in the morning and was back by night, having lunched lightly in the graveyard. But some days later, wishing to know his age at death, I had to return to the grave, to note the date of his birth. These two limiting dates I then jotted down on a piece of paper, which I now carry about with me. I am thus in a position to affirm that I must have been about twenty-five at the time of my marriage. For the date of my own birth, I repeat, my own birth, I have never forgotten, I never had to note it down, it remains graven in my memory, the year at least, in figures that life will not easily erase. The day itself comes back to me, when I put my mind to it, and I often celebrate it, after my fashion, I don't say each time it comes back, for it comes back too often, but often.

Personally I have no bone to pick with graveyards, I take the air there willingly, perhaps more willingly than elsewhere, when take the air I must. The smell of corpses, distinctly perceptible under those of grass and humus mingled, I do not find unpleasant, a trifle on the sweet side perhaps, a trifle heady, but how infinitely preferable to what the living emit, their feet, teeth, armpits, arses, sticky foreskins and frustrated ovules. And when my father's remains join in, however modestly, I can almost shed a tear. The living wash in vain, in vain perfume themselves, they stink. Yes, as a place for an outing, when out I must, leave me my graveyards and keep—you—to your public parks and

61

beauty-spots. My sandwich, my banana, taste sweeter when I'm sitting on a tomb, and when the time comes to piss again, as it so often does, I have my pick. Or I wander, hands clasped behind my back, among the slabs, the flat, the leaning and the upright, culling the inscriptions. Of these I never weary, there are always three or four of such drollery that I have to hold on to the cross, or the stele, or the angel, so as not to fall. Mine I composed long since and am still pleased with it, tolerably pleased. My other writings are no sooner dry than they revolt me, but my epitaph still meets with my approval. There is little chance unfortunately of its ever being reared above the skull that conceived it, unless the State takes up the matter. But to be unearthed I must first be found, and I greatly fear those gentlemen will have as much trouble finding me dead as alive. So I hasten to record it here and now, while there is yet time:

> Hereunder lies the above who up below
> So hourly died that he lived on till now.

The second and last or rather latter line limps a little perhaps, but that is no great matter, I'll be forgiven more than that when I'm forgotten. Then with a little luck you hit on a genuine interment, with real live mourners and the odd relict trying to throw herself into the pit. And nearly always that charming business with the dust, though in my experience there is nothing less dusty than holes of this type, verging on muck for the most part, nor anything particularly powdery about the deceased, unless he happened to have died, or she, by fire. No matter, their little gimmick with the dust is charming. But my father's yard was not amongst my favourite. To begin with it was too remote, way out in the wilds of the country on the side of a hill, and too small, far too small, to go on with. Indeed it was almost full, a few more widows and they'd be turning them away. I infinitely preferred Ohlsdorf, particularly the Linne section, on Prussian soil, with its nine hundred acres of corpses packed tight, though I knew no one there, except by reputation the wild animal collector Hagenbeck. A lion, if I remember right, is carved on his monument, death must have had for Hagenbeck the countenance of a lion. Coaches ply to and fro, crammed with widows, widowers, orphans and the like. Groves, grottoes, artificial lakes with swans, offer consolation to the inconsolable. It was December, I had never felt so cold, the eel soup lay heavy on my stomach, I was afraid I'd die, I turned aside to vomit, I envied them.

But to pass on to less melancholy matters, on my father's death I had to leave the house. It was he who wanted me in the house. He was a strange man. One day he said, Leave him alone, he's not disturbing anyone. He didn't know I was listening. This was a view he must often have voiced, but the other times I wasn't by. They would never let me see his will, they simply said he had left me such a sum. I believed then and still believe he had stipulated in his will that I be left the room I had occupied in his lifetime and food brought me there, as hitherto. He may even have given this the force of condition precedent. Presumably he liked to feel me under his roof, otherwise he would not have opposed my eviction. Perhaps he merely pitied me. But somehow I think not. He should have left me the entire house, then I'd have been all right, the others too for that matter, I'd have summoned them and said, Stay, stay by all means, your home is here. Yes, he was properly had, my poor father, if his purpose was really to go on protecting me from beyond the tomb. With regard to the money it is only fair to say they gave it to me without delay, on the very day following the inhumation. Perhaps they were legally bound to. I said to them, Keep this money and let me live on here, in my room, as in Papa's lifetime. I added, God rest his soul, in the hope of melting them. But they refused. I offered to place myself at their disposal, a few hours every day, for the little odd maintenance jobs every dwelling requires, if it is not to crumble away. Pottering is still just possible, I don't know why. I proposed in particular to look after the hothouse. There I would have gladly whiled away the hours, in the heat, tending the tomatoes, hyacinths, pinks and seedlings. My father and I alone, in that

63

household, understood tomatoes. But they refused. One day, on my return from stool, I found my room locked and my belongings in a heap before the door. This will give you some idea how constipated I was, at that juncture. It was, I am now convinced, anxiety constipation. But was I genuinely constipated? Somehow I think not. Softly, softly. And yet I must have been, for how otherwise account for those long, those cruel sessions in the necessary house? At such times I never read, any more than at other times, never gave way to revery or meditation, just gazed dully at the almanac hanging from a nail before my eyes, with its chromo of a bearded stripling in the midst of sheep, Jesus no doubt, parted the cheeks with both hands and strained, heave! ho! heave! ho!, with the motions of one tugging at the oar, and only one thought in my mind, to be back in my room and flat on my back again. What can that have been but constipation? Or am I confusing it with diarrhoea? It's all a muddle in my head, graves and nuptials and the different varieties of motion. Of my scanty belongings they had made a little heap, on the floor, against the door. I can still see that little heap, in the kind of recess full of shadow between the landing and my room. It was in this narrow space, guarded on three sides only, that I had to change, I mean exchange my dressing-gown and nightgown for my travelling costume, I mean shoes, socks, trousers, shirt, coat, greatcoat and hat, I can think of nothing else. I tried other doors, turning the knobs and pushing, or pulling, before I left the house, but none yielded. I think if I'd found one open I'd have barricaded myself in the room, nothing less than gas would have dislodged me. I felt the house crammed as usual, the usual pack, but saw no one. I imagined them in their various rooms, all bolts drawn, every sense on the alert. Then the rush to the window, each holding back a little, hidden by the curtain, at the sound of the street door closing behind me, I should have left it open. Then the doors fly open and out they pour, men, women and children, and the voices, the sighs, the smiles, the hands, the keys in the hands, the blessed relief, the precautions rehearsed, if this then that, but if that then this, all clear and joy in every heart, come let's eat, the fumigation can wait. All imagination to be sure, I was already on my way, things may have passed quite differently, but who cares how things pass, provided they pass. All those lips that had kissed me, those hearts that had loved me (it is with the heart one loves, is it not, or am I confusing it with something else?), those hands that had played with mine and those minds that had almost made their own of me! Humans are truly strange. Poor Papa, a nice mug he must have felt that day if he could see me, see us, a nice mug on my account I mean. Unless in his great disembodied wisdom he saw further than his son whose corpse was not yet quite up to scratch.

But to pass on to less melancholy matters, the name of the woman with whom I was soon to be united was Lulu. So at least she assured me and I can't see what interest she could have had in lying to me, on this score. Of course one can never tell. She also disclosed her family name, but I've forgotten it. I should have made a note of it, on a piece of paper, I hate to forget a proper name. I met her on a bench, on the bank of the canal, one of the canals, for our town boasts two, though I never knew which was which. It was a well situated bench, backed by a mound of solid earth and garbage, so that my rear was covered. My flanks too, partially, thanks to a pair of venerable trees, more than venerable, dead, at either end of the bench. It was no doubt these trees one fine day, aripple with all their foliage, that had sown the idea of a bench, in someone's fancy. To the fore, a few yards away, flowed the canal, if canals flow, don't ask me, so that from that quarter too the risk of surprise was small. And yet she surprised me. I lay stretched out, the night being warm, gazing up through the bare boughs interlocking high above me, where the trees clung together for support, and through the drifting cloud, at a patch of starry sky as it came and went. Shove up, she said. My first movement was to go, but my fatigue, and my having nowhere to go, dissuaded me from acting on it. So I drew back my feet a little way and she sat. Nothing more passed between us that evening and she soon took herself off, without another word. All she had done was sing, beneath her breath, as to herself, and without the words fortunately, some old folk songs, and so disjointedly, skipping from one to another and finishing none, that even I found it strange. The voice, though out of tune, was not unpleasant. It breathed of a soul too soon wearied ever to conclude, that perhaps least arse-aching soul of all. The bench itself was soon more than she could bear and as for me, one look had been enough for her. Whereas in reality she was a most tenacious woman. She came back next day and the day after and all went off more or less as before. Perhaps a few words were exchanged. The next day it was raining and I felt in security. Wrong again. I asked her if she was resolved to disturb me every evening. I disturb you? she said. I felt her eyes on me. They can't have seen much, two eyelids at the most, with a hint of nose and brow, darkly, because of the dark. I thought we were easy, she said. You disturb me, I said, I can't stretch out with you there. The collar of my greatcoat was over my mouth and yet she heard me. Must you stretch out? she said. The mistake one makes is to speak to people. You have only to put your feet on my knees, she said. I didn't wait to be asked twice, under my miserable calves I felt her fat thighs. She began stroking my ankles. I considered kicking her in the cunt. You speak to people about stretching out and they immediately see a body at full length. What mattered to me in my dispeopled kingdom, that in regard to which the disposition of my carcass was the merest and most futile of accidents, was supineness in the mind, the dulling of the self and of that residue of execrable frippery known as the non-self and even the world, for short. But man is still today, at the age of twenty-five, at the mercy of an erection, physically too, from time to time, it's the common lot, even I was not immune, if that may be called an erection. It did not escape her naturally, women smell a rigid phallus ten miles away and wonder, How on earth did he spot me from there? One is no longer onself, on such occasions, and it is painful to be no longer oneself, even more painful if possible than when one is.

For when one is one knows what to do to be less so, whereas when one is not one is any old one irredeemably. What goes by the name of love is banishment, with now and then a postcard from the homeland, such is my considered opinion, this evening. When she had finished and my self been resumed, mine own, the mitigable, with the help of a brief torpor, it was alone. I sometimes wonder if that is not all invention, if in reality things did not take quite a different course, one I had no choice but to forget. And yet her image remains bound, for me, to that of the bench, not the bench by day, nor yet the bench by night, but the bench at evening, in such sort that to speak of the bench, as it appeared to me at evening, is to speak of her, for me. That proves nothing, but there is nothing I wish to prove. On the subject of the bench by day no words need be wasted, it never knew me, gone before morning and never back till dusk. Yes, in the daytime I foraged for food and marked down likely cover. Were you to inquire, as undoubtedly you itch, what I had done with the money my father had left me, the answer would be I had done nothing with it but leave it lie in my pocket. For I knew I would not be always young, and that summer does not last for ever either, nor even autumn, my mean soul told me so. In the end I told her I'd had enough. She disturbed me exceedingly, even absent. Indeed she still disturbs me, but no worse now than the rest. And it matters nothing to me now, to be disturbed, or so little, what does it mean, disturbed, and what would I do with myself if I wasn't? Yes, I've changed my system, it's the winning one at last, for the ninth or tenth time, not to mention not long now, not long till curtain down, on disturbers and disturbed, no more tattle about that, all that, her and the others, the shitball and heaven's high halls. So you don't want me to come any more, she said. It's incredible the way they repeat what you've just said to them, as if they risked faggot and fire in believing their ears. I told her to come just the odd time. I didn't understand women at that period. I still don't for that matter. Nor men either. Nor animals either. What I understand best, which is not saying much, are my pains. I think them through daily, it doesn't take long, thought moves so fast, but they are not only in my thought, not all. Yes, there are moments, particularly in the afternoon, when I go all syncretist, à la Reinhold. What equilibrium! But even them, my pains, I understand ill. That must come from my not being all pain and nothing else. There's the rub. Then they recede, or I, till they fill me with amaze and wonder, seen from a better planet. Not often, but I ask no more. Catch-cony life! To be nothing but pain, how that would simplify matters! Omnidolent! Impious dream. I'll tell them to you some day none the less, if I think of it, if I can, my strange pains, in detail, distinguishing between the different kinds, for the sake of clarity, those of the mind, those of the heart or emotional conative, those of the soul (none prettier than these) and finally those of the frame proper, first the inner or latent, then those affecting the surface, beginning with the hair and scalp and moving methodically down, without haste, all the way down to the feet beloved of the corn, the cramp, the kibe, the bunion, the hammer toe, the nail ingrown, the fallen arch, the common blain, the club foot, duck foot, goose foot, pigeon foot, flat foot, trench foot and other curiosities. And I'll tell by the same token, for those kind enough to listen, in accordance with a system whose inventor I forget, of those instants when, neither drugged, nor drunk, nor in ecstasy, one feels nothing. Next of course she desired to know what I meant by the odd time, that's what you get for opening your mouth. Once a week? Once in ten days? Once a fortnight? I replied less often, far less often, less often to the point of no more if she could, and if she could not the least often possible. And the next day (what is more) I abandoned the bench, less I must confess on her account than on its, for the site no longer answered my requirements, modest though they were, now that the air was beginning to strike chill, and for other reasons better not wasted on cunts like you, and took refuge in a deserted cowshed marked on one of my forays. It stood in the corner of a field richer on the surface in nettles than in grass and in mud than in nettles, but whose subsoil was perhaps possessed of exceptional qualities. It was in this byre, littered with dry and hollow cowclaps subsiding with a sigh at the poke of my finger, that for the first time in my life, and I would not hesitate to say the last if I had not to husband my cyanide, I had to contend with a feeling which gradually assumed, to my dismay, the dread name of love. What constitutes the charm of our country, apart of course from its scant population, and this without help of the meanest contraceptive, is that all is derelict, with the sole exception of history's ancient faeces. These are ardently sought after, stuffed and carried in procession. Wherever nauseated time has dropped a nice fat turd you will find our patriots, sniffing it up on all fours, their faces on fire. Elysium of the roofless. Hence my happiness at last. Lie down, all seems to say, lie down and stay down. I see no connexion between these remarks. But that one exists, and even more than one, I have little doubt, for my part. But what? Which? Yes, I loved her, it's the name I gave, still give alas, to what I was doing then. I had nothing to go by, having never loved before, but of course had heard of the thing, at home, at school, in brothel and at church, and read romances, in prose and verse, under the guidance of my tutor, in six or seven languages, both dead and living, in which it was handled at length. I was therefore in a position, in spite of all, to put a label on what I was about when I found myself inscribing the letters of Lulu in an old heifer pat or flat on my face in the mud under the moon trying to tear up the nettles by the roots. They were giant nettles some full three foot high, to tear them up assuaged my pain, and yet it's not like me to do that to weeds, on the contrary, I'd smother them in manure if I had any. Flowers are a different matter. Love brings out the worst in man and no error. But what kind of love was this, exactly? Love-passion? Somehow I think not. That's the priapic one, is it not? Or is this a different variety? There are so many, are there not? All equally if not more delicious, are they not? Platonic love, for example, there's another just occurs to me. It's disinterested. Perhaps I loved her with a platonic love? But somehow I think not. Would I have been tracing her name in old cowshit if my love had been pure and disinterested? And with my devil's finger into the bargain, which I then sucked. Come now! My thoughts were all of Lulu, if that doesn't give you some idea nothing will. Anyhow I'm sick and tired of this name Lulu, I'll give her another, more like her, Anna for example, it's not more like her but no matter. I thought of Anna then, I who had learnt to think of nothing, nothing except my pains, a quick think through, and of what steps to take not to perish offhand of hunger, or cold, or shame, but never on any account of living beings as such (I wonder what that means) whatever I may have said, or may still say, to the contrary or otherwise, on this subject. But I have always spoken, no doubt always shall, of things that never existed, or that existed if you insist, no doubt always will, but not with the existence I ascribe to them. Kepis, for example, exist beyond a doubt, indeed there is little hope of their ever disappearing, but personally I never wore a kepi. I wrote somewhere, They gave me . . . a hat. Now the truth is they never gave me a hat, I have always had my own hat, the one my father gave me, and I have never had any other hat than that hat. I may add it has followed me to the grave. I thought of Anna then, long long sessions, twenty minutes, twenty-five minutes and even as long as half an hour daily. I obtain these figures by the addition of other, lesser figures. That must have been my way of loving. Are we to infer from this I loved her with that intellectual love which drew from me such drivel, in another place? Somehow I think not. For had my love been of this kind would I have stooped to inscribe the letters of Anna in time's forgotten cowpats? To divellicate urtica *plenis manibus*? And felt, under my tossing head, her thighs to bounce like so many demon bolsters? Come now! In order to put an end, to try and put an end, to this plight, I returned one evening to the bench, at the hour she had used to join me there. There was no sign of her and I waited in vain. It was December already, if not January, and the cold was seasonable, that is to say reasonable, like all that is seasonable. But one is the hour of the dial, and another that of changing air and sky, and another yet again the heart's. To this thought, once back in the straw, I owed an excellent night. The next day I was earlier to the bench, much earlier, night having barely fallen, winter night, and yet too late, for she was there already, on the bench, under the boughs tinkling with rime, her back to the frosted mound, facing the icy water. I told you she was a highly tenacious woman. I felt nothing. What interest could she have in pursuing me thus? I asked her, without sitting down, stumping to and fro. The cold had embossed the path. She replied she didn't know. What could she see in me, would she kindly tell me that at least, if she could. She replied she couldn't. She seemed warmly clad, her hands buried in a muff. As I looked at this muff, I remember, tears came to my eyes. And yet I forget what colour it was. The state I was in then! I have always wept freely, without the least benefit to myself, till recently. If I had to weep this minute I could squeeze till I was blue, I'm convinced not a drop would fall. The state I am in now! It was things made me weep. And yet I felt no sorrow. When I found myself in tears for no apparent reason it meant I had caught sight of something unbeknownst. So I wonder if it was really the muff that evening, if it was not rather the path, so iron hard and bossy as perhaps to feel like cobbles to my tread, or some other thing, some chance thing glimpsed below the threshold, that so unmanned me. As for her, I might as well never have laid eyes on her before. She sat all huddled and muffled up, her head sunk, the muff with her hands in her lap, her legs pressed tight together, her heels clear of the ground. Shapeless, ageless, almost lifeless, it might have been anything or anyone, an old woman or a little girl. And the way she kept on saying, I don't know, I can't. I alone did not know and could not. Is it on my account you came? I said. She managed yes to that. Well here I am, I said. And I? Had I not come on hers? Here we are, I said. I sat down beside her but sprang up again immediately as though scalded. I longed to be gone, to know if it was over. But before going, to be on the safe side, I asked her to sing me a song. I thought at first she was going to refuse, I mean simply not sing, but no, after a moment she began to sing and sang for some time, all the time the same song it seemed to me, without change of attitude. I did not know the song, I had never heard it before and shall never hear it again. It had something to do with lemon trees, or orange trees, I forget, that is all I remember, and for me that is no mean feat, to remember it had something to do with lemon trees, or orange trees, I forget, for of all the other songs I have ever heard in my life, and I have heard plenty, it being apparently impossible, physically impossible short of being deaf, to get through this world, even my way, without hearing singing, I have retained nothing, not a word, not a note, or so few words, so few notes, that, that what, that nothing, this sentence has gone on long enough. Then I started to go and as I went I heard her singing another song, or perhaps more verses of the same, fainter and fainter the further I went, then no more, either because she had come to an end or because I was gone too far to hear her. To have to harbour such a doubt was something I preferred to avoid, at that period. I lived of course in doubt, on doubt, but such trivial doubts as this, purely somatic as some say, were best cleared up without delay, they could nag at me like gnats for weeks on end. So I retraced my steps a little way and stopped. At first I heard nothing, then the voice again, but only just, so faintly did it carry. First I didn't hear it, then I did, I must therefore have begun hearing it, at a certain point, but no, there was no beginning, the sound emerged so softly from the silence and so resembled it. When the voice ceased at last I approached a little nearer, to make sure it had really ceased and not merely been lowered. Then in despair, saying, No knowing, no knowing, short of being beside her, bent over her, I turned on my heel and went, for good, full of doubt. But some weeks later, even more dead than alive than usual, I returned to the bench, for the fourth or fifth time since I had abandoned it, at roughly the same hour, I mean roughly the same sky, no, I don't mean that either, for it's always the same sky and never the same sky, what words are there for that, none I know, period. She wasn't there, then suddenly she was, I don't know how, I didn't

see her come, nor hear her, all ears and eyes though I was. Let
us say it was raining, nothing like a change, if only of weather.
She had her umbrella up, naturally, what an outfit. I asked if
she came every evening. No, she said, just the odd time. The
bench was soaking wet, we paced up and down, not daring to
sit. I took her arm, out of curiosity, to see if it would give me
pleasure, it gave me none, I let it go. But why these particulars.
To put off the evil hour. I saw her face a little clearer, it seemed
normal to me, a face like millions of others. The eyes were
crooked, but I didn't know that till later. It looked neither young
nor old, the face, as though stranded between the vernal and the
sere. Such ambiguity I found difficult to bear, at that period. As
to whether it was beautiful, the face, or had once been beautiful, or could conceivably become beautiful, I confess I could
form no opinion. I had seen faces in photographs I might have
found beautiful had I known even vaguely in what beauty was
supposed to consist. And my father's face, on his death-bolster,
had seemed to hint at some form of aesthetics relevant to man.
But the faces of the living, all grimace and flush, can they be
described as objects? I admired in spite of the dark, in spite of
my fluster, the way still or scarcely flowing water reaches up, as
though athirst, to that falling from the sky. She asked if I would
like her to sing something. I replied no, I would like her to say
something. I thought she would say she had nothing to say, it
would have been like her, and so was agreeably surprised when
she said she had a room, most agreeably surprised, though I
suspected as much. Who has not a room? Ah I hear the clamour.
I have two rooms, she said. Just how many rooms do you have?
I said. She said she had two rooms and a kitchen. The premises
were expanding steadily, given time she would remember a
bathroom. Is it two rooms I heard you say? I said. Yes, she said.
Adjacent? I said. At last conversation worthy of the name.
Separated by the kitchen, she said. I asked her why she had not
told me before. I must have been beside myself, at this period.
I did not feel easy when I was with her, but at least free to think
of something else than her, of the old trusty things, and so little

73

by little, as down steps towards a deep, of nothing. And I knew that away from her I would forfeit this freedom.

There were in fact two rooms, separated by a kitchen, she had not lied to me. She said I should have fetched my things. I explained I had no things. It was at the top of an old house, with a view of the mountains for those who cared. She lit an oil-lamp. You have no current? I said. No, she said, but I have running water and gas. Ha, I said, you have gas. She began to undress. When at their wit's end they undress, no doubt the wisest course. She took off everything, with a slowness fit to enflame an elephant, except her stockings, calculated presumably to bring my concupiscence to the boil. It was then I noticed the squint. Fortunately she was not the first naked woman to have crossed my path, so I could stay, I knew she would not explode. I asked to see the other room which I had not yet seen. If I had seen it already I would have asked to see it again. Will you not undress? she said. Oh you know, I said, I seldom undress. It was the truth. I was never one to undress indiscriminately. I often took off my boots when I went to bed, I mean when I composed myself (composed!) to sleep, not to mention this or that outer garment according to the outer temperature. She was therefore obliged, out of common savoir faire, to throw on a wrap and light me the way. We went via the kitchen. We could just as well have gone via the corridor, as I realized later, but we went via the kitchen, I don't know why, perhaps it was the shorter way. I surveyed the room with horror. Such density of furniture defeats imagination. Not a doubt, I must have seen that room somewhere. What's this? I cried. The parlour, she said. The parlour! I began putting out the furniture through the door to the corridor. She watched, in sorrow I suppose, but not necessarily. She asked me what I was doing. She can't have expected an answer. I put it out piece by piece, and even two at a time, and stacked it all up in the corridor, against the outer wall. There were hundreds of pieces, large and small, in the end they blocked the door, making egress impossible, and *a fortiori* ingress, to and from the corridor. The door could be opened and closed, since it opened inwards, but had become impassable. To put it mildly. At least take off your hat, she said. I'll treat of my hat some other time perhaps. Finally the room was empty but for a sofa and some shelves fixed to the wall. The former I dragged to the back of the room, near the door, and next day took down the latter and put them out, in the corridor, with the rest. As I was taking them down, strange memory, I heard the word fibrome, or brone, I don't know which, never knew, never knew what it meant and never had the curiosity to find out. The things one recalls! and records! When all was in order at last I dropped on the sofa. She had not raised her little finger to help me. I'll get sheets and blankets, she said. But I wouldn't hear of sheets. You couldn't draw the curtain? I said. The window was frosted over. The effect was not white, because of the night, but faintly luminous none the less. This faint cold sheen, though I lay with my feet towards the door, was more than I could bear. I suddenly rose and changed the position of the sofa, that is to say turned it round so that the back, hitherto against the wall, was now on the outside and consequently the front, or way in, on the inside. Then I climbed back, like a dog into its basket. I'll leave you the lamp, she said, but I begged her to take it with her. And suppose you need something in the night, she said. She was going to start quibbling again, I could feel it. Do you know where the convenience is? she said. She was right, I was forgetting. To relieve oneself in bed is enjoyable at the time, but soon a source of discomfort. Give me a chamber-pot, I said. But she did not possess one. I have a close-stool of sorts, she said. I saw the grandmother on it, sitting up very stiff and grand, having just purchased it, pardon, picked it up, at a charity sale, or perhaps won it in a raffle, a period piece, and now trying it out, doing her best rather, almost wishing someone could see her. That's the idea, proscrastinate. Any old recipient, I said, I don't have the flux. She came back with a kind of saucepan, not a true saucepan for it had no handle, it was oval in shape with two lugs and a lid. My stewpan, she said. I don't need the lid, I said. You don't need the lid? she said. If I had said I needed the lid she

75

would have said, You need the lid? I drew this utensil down under the blanket, I like something in my hand when sleeping, it reassures me, and my hat was still wringing. I turned to the wall. She caught up the lamp off the mantelpiece where she had set it down, that's the idea, every particular, it flung her waving shadow over me, I thought she was off, but no, she came stooping down towards me over the sofa back. All family possessions, she said. I in her shoes would have tiptoed away, but not she, not a stir. Already my love was waning, that was all that mattered. Yes, already I felt better, soon I'd be up to the slow descents again, the long submersions, so long denied me through her fault. And I had only just moved in! Try and put me out now, I said. I seemed not to grasp the meaning of these words, nor even hear the brief sound they made, till some seconds after having uttered them. I was so unused to speech that my mouth would sometimes open, of its own accord, and vent some phrase or phrases, grammatically unexceptionable but entirely devoid if not of meaning, for on close inspection they would reveal one, and even several, at least of foundation. But I heard each word no sooner spoken. Never had my voice taken so long to reach me as on this occasion. I turned over on my back to see what was going on. She was smiling. A little later she went away, taking the lamp with her. I heard her steps in the kitchen and then the door of her room close behind her. Why behind her? I was alone at last, in the dark at last. Enough about that. I thought I was all set for a good night, in spite of the strange surroundings, but no, my night was most agitated. I woke next morning quite worn out, my clothes in disorder, the blanket likewise, and Anna beside me, naked naturally. One shudders to think of her exertions. I still had the stewpan in my grasp. It had not served. I looked at my member. If only it could have spoken! Enough about that. It was my night of love.

Gradually I settled down, in this house. She brought my meals at the appointed hours, looked in now and then to see if all was well and make sure I needed nothing, emptied the stewpan once a day and did out the room once a month. She could not always resist the temptation to speak to me, but on the whole gave me no cause to complain. Sometimes I heard her singing in her room, the song traversed her door, then the kitchen, then my door, and in this way won to me, faint but indisputable. Unless it travelled by the corridor. This did not greatly incommode me, this occasional sound of singing. One day I asked her to bring me a hyacinth, live, in a pot. She brought it and put it on the mantelpiece, now the only place in my room to put things, unless you put them on the floor. Not a day passed without my looking at it. At first all went well, it even put forth a bloom or two, then it gave up and was soon no more than a limp stem hung with limp leaves. The bulb, half clear of the clay as though in search of oxygen, smelt foul. She wanted to remove it, but I told her to leave it. She wanted to get me another, but I told her I didn't want another. I was more seriously disturbed by other sounds, stifled giggles and groans, which filled the dwelling at certain hours of the night, and even of the day. I had given up thinking of her, quite given up, but still I needed silence, to live my life. In vain I tried to listen to such reasonings as that air is made to carry the clamours of the world, including inevitably much groan and giggle, I obtained no relief. I couldn't make out if it was always the same gent or more than one. Lovers' groans are so alike, and lovers' giggles. I had such horror then of these paltry perplexities that I always fell into the same error, that of seeking to clear them up. It took me a long time, my lifetime so to speak, to realize that the colour of an eye half seen, or the source of some distant sound, are closer to Giudecca in the hell of unknowing than the existence of God, or the origins of protoplasm, or the existence of self, and even less worthy than these to occupy the wise. It's a bit much, a lifetime, to achieve this consoling conclusion, it doesn't leave you much time to profit by it. So a fat lot of help it was when, having put the question to her, I was told they were clients she received in rotation. I could obviously have got up and gone to look through the keyhole. But what can you see, I ask you, through holes the likes of those? So you live by prostitution, I said. We live by prostitution, she said. You couldn't ask them to make less noise? I said, as if I believed her. I added, Or a different kind of noise. They can't help but yap and yelp, she said. I'll have to leave, I said. She found some old hangings in the family junk and hung them before our doors, hers and mine. I asked her if it would not be possible, now and then, to have a parsnip. A parsnip! she cried, as if I had asked for a dish of sucking Jew. I reminded her that the parsnip season was fast drawing to a close and that if, before it finally got there, she could feed me nothing but parsnips I'd be grateful. I like parsnips because they taste like violets and violets because they smell like parsnips. Were there no parsnips on earth violets would leave me cold and if violets did not exist I would care as little for parsnips as I do for turnips, or radishes. And even in the present state of their flora, I mean on this planet where parsnips and violets contrive to coexist, I could do without both with the utmost ease, the uttermost ease. One day she had the impudence to announce she was with child, and four or five months gone into the bargain, by me of all people! She offered me a side view of her belly. She even undressed, no doubt to prove she wasn't hiding a cushion under her skirt, and then of course for the pure pleasure of undressing. Perhaps it's just wind, I said, by way of consolation. She gazed at me with her big eyes whose colour I forget, with one big eye rather, for the other seemed riveted on the remains of the hyacinth. The more naked she was the more cross-eyed. Look, she said, stooping over her breasts, the haloes are darkening already. I summoned up my remaining strength and said, Abort, abort, and they'll blush like new. She had drawn back the curtain for a clear view of all her rotundities. I saw the mountain, impassable, cavernous, secret, where from morning to night I'd hear nothing but the wind, the curlews, the clink like distant silver of the stonecutters' hammers. I'd come out in the daytime to the heather and gorse, all warmth and scent, and watch at night the distant city lights, if I chose, and the other lights, the lighthouses and lightships my father had named for me, when

I was small, and whose names I could find again, in my memory, if I chose, that I knew. From that day forth things went from bad to worse, to worse and worse. Not that she neglected me, she could never have neglected me enough, but the way she kept plaguing me with *our* child, exhibiting her belly and breasts and saying it was due any moment, she could feel it lepping already. If it's lepping, I said, it's not mine. I might have been worse off than I was, in that house, that was certain, it fell short of my ideal naturally, but I wasn't blind to its advantages. I hesitated to leave, the leaves were falling already, I dreaded the winter. One should not dread the winter, it too has its bounties, the snow gives warmth and deadens the tumult and its pale days are soon over. But I did not yet know, at that time, how tender the earth can be for those who have only her and how many graves in her giving, for the living. What finished me was the birth. It woke me up. What that infant must have been going through! I fancy she had a woman with her, I seemed to hear steps in the kitchen, on and off. It went to my heart to leave a house without being put out. I crawled out over the back of the sofa, put on my coat, greatcoat and hat, I can think of nothing else, laced up my boots and opened the door to the corridor. A mass of junk barred my way, but I scrabbled and barged my way through it in the end, regardless of the clatter. I used the word marriage, it was a kind of union in spite of all. Precautions would have been superfluous, there was no competing with those cries. It must have been her first. They pursued me down the stairs and out into the street. I stopped before the house door and listened. I could still hear them. If I had not known there was crying in the house I might not have heard them. But knowing it I did. I was not sure where I was. I looked among the stars and constellations for the Wains, but could not find them. And yet they must have been there. My father was the first to show them to me. He had shown me others, but alone, without him beside me, I could never find any but the Wains. I began playing with the cries, a little in the same way as I had played with the song, on, back, on, back, if that may be called playing.

As long as I kept walking I didn't hear them, because of the footsteps. But as soon as I halted I heard them again, a little fainter each time, admittedly, but what does it matter, faint or loud, cry is cry, all that matters is that it should cease. For years I thought they would cease. Now I don't think so any more. I could have done with other loves perhaps. But there it is, either you love or you don't.